THE
SOUVENIR
MUSEUM

ELIZABETH
McCRACKEN

JONATHAN CAPE
LONDON

1 3 5 7 9 10 8 6 4 2

Jonathan Cape, an imprint of Vintage, is part of the Penguin Random House group of companies whose addresses can be found at global.penguinrandomhouse.com.

Penguin
Random House
UK

First published by Jonathan Cape in 2021

penguin.co.uk/vintage

A CIP catalogue record for this book is available from the British Library

ISBN 9781787333628

Designed by Paula Russell Szafranski

Printed and bound in Great Britain by Clays Ltd, Elcograf S.p.A.

The authorised representative in the EEA is Penguin Random House Ireland, Morrison Chambers, 32 Nassau Street, Dublin DO2 YH68

Penguin Random House is committed to a sustainable future for our business, our readers and our planet. This book is made from Forest Stewardship Council® certified paper.

MIX
Paper from
responsible sources
FSC
www.fsc.org   FSC® C018179

For my mother's sister, Carolyn Matulef,

and my father's sister, Elizabeth Wrede McCracken

Map of Itself

The idea of travel. The very idea.

—Brenda Shaughnessy, *The Octopus Museum*

CONTENTS

THE IRISH WEDDING

Because Jack didn't drive—not stick, not on the left side of the road, not at all ever—Sadie piloted the rental car from the Dublin airport to the wedding, grinding gears and scraping along the greenery and—for a few miles—creeping behind a tractor on a winding road. It was ten p.m. and raining. If Ireland was emerald she couldn't say. The tractor was a comfort, lit up with white lights, which she planned to follow as long as she could. Till dawn if necessary.

"Pass him," said Jack.

"You pass him," said Sadie.

"I'm not driving."

"That's right," said Sadie.

Not their wedding but Jack's middle older sister Fiona's. Sadie would meet the entire family today, simultaneously: Fiona and her Dutch about-to-be-husband, Piet; his youngest older sister, Katie, and his oldest older sister, Eloise, and their families; and, of course, his parents, the significant Mister and Missus, Michael and Irene Valerts. Jack was the youngest of all of them, the only one born in America—not American, he insisted, despite his American accent. Everyone else in his family was English. He was, too, though he couldn't pass.

Sadie drove as an act of heroism, though at any moment she might swerve off the road, into a ditch or off a cliff: she wasn't sure, she couldn't see. In Boston, where they lived, she almost never got a chance to drive, to perform this act of casual generosity. When she did, Jack was full of gratitude and compliments, passed her snacks and drinks, read to her from magazines. They were still in the early days of their lives together. This was their first wedding.

"You're a little close," said Jack. "To the side here."

He didn't drive, but his body acted as though it knew all about it. It braked and seized up and readied for death. The rental car was small, bright blue, a brand and model Sadie had never heard of, with some sort of winged scaly mythical creature in the middle of the steering wheel. The wedding would be in a large house near the town of Clonmel. The good news was that the house belonged to Fiona and Piet, who'd bought it for a song after its occupant had died in one of its many rooms, and so they would stay there for free. That was also the bad news, all those hours she would have to perform as herself in front of Jack's family. They had spent the day traveling, flying through the air and through time zones, and now it was the middle of the night.

"We'll miss supper," said Jack.

"We've missed it."

"We've missed it. That's all right."

The Irish winds pushed at the little car and Sadie leaned forward, as though the road itself were a map she couldn't read—no, not *as though*. It was.

"How are you doing?" asked Jack.

"I'm fine!" she said in a cheerful voice. The voice of her mother, she realized, who was terrifyingly cheerful when things were dire. From her mother she'd also accepted, unthinkingly, the advice that you should always buy the full car insurance when driving on the wrong side of the road, so she had, thank God, since the car was already scratched down one door and soon would lose its passenger wing mirror.

The tractor slowed them down, but so did Sadie's sense that in the dark Ireland was making itself up as it went along, Jack giving directions at the last minute, sometimes consulting a map and sometimes an old envelope upon which he'd written notes. Finally they arrived and pulled up the long drive. They could make out the dull shape of the dark house amid the trees and damp.

"It's a mansion," said Sadie.

"It's a Georgian cube," said Jack.

Outside the car the rain was friendlier than it had been on the car windows, over friendly, wet and insinuating, running its fingers through their hair and down the backs of their collars. They left their luggage and ran for the front door, which had a mammoth Dickensian knocker, ready to morph into somebody's face, but whose? Jack shouldered the door open. Then they were in a dim foyer illuminated by a night-light: a black-and-white Vermeer floor and five doors. It felt like a puzzle. There was a lion behind one of those doors, Sadie was sure, and a happy future behind another, and a lifetime supply of Rice-A-Roni behind a third.

The Rice-A-Roni door opened to reveal a small woman holding a flashlight, dressed like a stable boy, or what Sadie imagined was a stable boy, corduroy pants tucked into rubber boots, a sweater that looked handed down by a careless person with a lot of money: brown cashmere with unraveling cuffs.

"This way," she said in a stage whisper. "Hello!"

"Hello!" whispered Jack.

"We've put you in the snug, just for tonight," she whispered. "Hope that's all right. Tomorrow some family is shifting to the hotel downtown. You can take our room then."

They followed her to the middle of the house, to a tiny room filled with a bed. "Air mattress, but it's a good one. The electric blanket's on. Poor things," the woman said, "you must be *shattered*."

"We are," said Jack.

"We'll meet properly in the morning," the woman said. "Lenny, your hair's *hilarious*. It's quite big, isn't it."

He raised his hands and felt his head. "This is Sadie," he said.

"It's lovely to meet you, Sadie. See you in the morning." The woman went out a door opposite the door they'd come in. They could hear her tick away on the floorboards. Then the house was silent all around them.

"Why'd she call you Lenny?" asked Sadie.

"Because it's my name." He gave the air mattress a kick. "My actual name. Leonard. You know that. My family calls me Lenny. I hate it."

"I knew it was your name, but I didn't know it was your *name*," she said.

"I hate it," he repeated.

She felt wild with various discomforts. "I need to pee."

They were in a room with three doors: the one they'd come in; the door through which the woman had left; and a door to the outside with windowpanes. The rain seemed to patter at all of them.

"It's too confusing," said Jack. "Go outside."

"Go *outside*?" She opened the door they'd come through, only to be faced with half a dozen other doors, all closed. She might find a toilet behind any of them, or a sleeping stranger. Already Jack had opened the back door. "Well, I'm having a slash outdoors," he said.

"Easy for you to say."

"G'wan," he said. "G'wan, g'wan, g'wan."

Could be worse, she told herself. She was wearing tights and a dress, so she took off her coat and her tights and went out in the rain. It was cold, but she was cold—she could hardly get any colder.

"You done with your slash?" she asked.

"Done."

"Here, give me your hand. Is your entire family here?"

"I imagine."

"Are they watching me pee in the rain?"

"Without a doubt."

"Who was that lady?"

"That lady was the bride. Fiona. Did I not say?"

"You did not. Okay. Done."

Inside Jack found a little lamp to switch on, clamped to

the edge of a stepladder. The walls were vivid green, and he looked like a Toulouse-Lautrec lady, lit from underneath, glamorous, sure to die or go blind or mad.

The idea of an air mattress and an electric blanket had sounded like a disaster sandwich to Sadie, but she put on her underpants and took off her wet dress and used it to dry her wet knees, and then, cold to the bones, she slid in. She'd never slept under an electric blanket. It was warm, lulling, and she felt like a little abandoned animal whose mother has died but who yet might be saved by technology. *Incubated.* That's how she felt. Maybe she would be electrocuted, and maybe the air mattress would spring a leak and they would sail around the room as it emptied out. For the moment she had never felt anything more exquisite, this warm, buoyant raft heading out to sleep.

Mere hours later she heard the noise of children, and then a barking voice saying, "No, Thomas, *no*, they're asleep, no, Pie, *come here*, you'll play piano later." It was sodden daylight. The rain had stopped, but she could hear water dripping off things. Next to her was a paint-splattered upright piano. The electric blanket was cold. The air mattress had lost some air, but they were afloat upon it.

"Ireland," said Jack.

"Still?" said Sadie.

"Yes, and for days."

She fell back asleep.

As she woke the next time she could hear voices behind all the doors, left, right, at the head of the bed. She was in her underwear, locked in a secret room surrounded by Jack's family. By God, she should have passed that tractor, been braver, driven right past Clonmel to the Dingle Peninsula on the other side of the country. *Dingle*. What a name for a beautiful place. She had never been there, but a high school friend had once sent her a postcard from the beach of Inch.

"*Jack*," she said. Jack wasn't there. He was already out, goddamn him. She said, to herself, in a whisper, "Lenny."

No curtains at the back. But he'd spread out her dress on the ladder, and it was halfway dry, and she put it on and stood next to the mattress—she had to tick her toes beneath to fit—and listened for his voice. There it was, and the sound of pouring coffee. Or pouring tea. She hoped it was coffee. He was talking to other people. She couldn't possibly go out there. Perhaps if she went out the other way, she could find her way to the car and her luggage and a toothbrush.

Behind the door was the black-and-white hallway. At the front of the house a barefoot man looked out a window. He turned to her. He wasn't English—something about the spikiness of his haircut and the severity of his square steel glasses. He had a sandwich in his hand. "Hallo," he said, and then, in a calm European voice, "Did you mean to leave the car door open?"

"What? No!"

"There is a cat and a dog," he said. "Inside your car."

Her shoes were by the door, damp as oysters. She put them on and winced. "A cat and dog," she said. It had been raining cats and dogs: she believed he spoke metaphorically. But he didn't. The driver's-side door was open, and then a Shetland sheepdog jumped out onto the drive. Already a

Siamese cat was picking its way along the cobblestone toward the front garden.

"So you see," said the man, who had followed in his bare feet. He closed the car door for her. "I'm Piet."

"Sadie," she said. "Are—is that *your* dog?"

"Neighbor's, maybe? I don't know. Not yours? You didn't bring us a cat and a dog from America?"

In the daylight she could see that they were at the top of a hill, other hills in front of her in various degrees of fog and sparkle. "Do you think they spent the whole night there?"

Piet nodded. "I like to think so, yes."

"Like a children's book," she said. The embarrassed feeling of having been so exhausted that she'd left the door open in a rainstorm evaporated. Where else would the animals of Clonmel take shelter? It must be a good sign. An odd and happy marriage, after all. But whose sign was it?

Piet ripped his sandwich in two and handed the unbitten portion to her. "Breakfast," he said. Dizzily, she bit into it. She had been expecting ham, but it was sweet and delicious and crunched under her teeth.

"Strawberry," said Piet. "Butter, sugar." He felt his chin. "I suppose I am getting married and should shave."

"The wedding's here?"

"The wedding's at church," he said philosophically. "I could be married on a rock, by a buzzard or a bear, but not Fiona. She believes in God. God is everywhere, I told her, don't you think? But I am an atheist, and so my opinions on God do not matter."

He carried her bag into the house and pointed her to

the bathroom, which had a toilet unconvincingly attached to the wall and a claw-foot tub belly-up in the corner, awaiting its installation. The sink worked. Her toothbrush had rubbed up against something soapy in the cosmetic bag, and it tasted like mint and perfume and incompetence. She pulled on a clean dress, a pair of leggings, clean socks, draped her dirty damp clothing over the top, stowed the suitcase in the snug, and went around the other way to follow the sound of voices to a kitchen. There was Jack leaning against a yellow enameled stove, surrounded by English people, all of them dressed like stable hands. Him, too, in yesterday's clothing. By sleeping in it he seemed to have achieved the correct level of rumpled. The room smelled of cigarettes and sausage. She studied Jack's face for some evidence of guilt over abandoning her.

Instead he said, "There she is!"

She went to him, but he did not—as he would in America—put his arm around her. "Sit," he said to her, his voice full of kindness, she could tell how happy he was to see her, "sit, sit. What can I get you? Let me make you some coffee. This is Sadie," he said to the English people. They were all women, with the exception of one small boy who abruptly opened the door to the snug and went to bang on the piano and a man with giant hands who was putting away dishes in a cupboard. These were people who called Jack Lenny. They looked just the sort. "Sadie: you've met Fiona, and here's Katie and Eloise, my other sisters. That's Katie's husband, Paul."

Together Jack and his sisters looked like the full toolbox:

hatchet, knife, spade, trowel. Sadie, having been sat, understood that she was not to make physical contact with any of the people present. She was about to say hello when an older man came through a door in the corner, shaking water from his hands.

Jack's father. It had to be. He had Jack's thick curls, though whiter and tidier. He was a tall man, serrated—Sadie felt cut already, as she would always feel around him—with extraordinarily blue eyes he must have been vain about. He wore a sweater one shade darker—peacock—to bring them out.

"Still there!" he said in a jubilant voice.

"For fuck's sake," said Jack.

"It's *not*!" said the woman who'd let them in. Fiona. The bride. She was washing dishes and smoking a cigarette. "It can't be."

"Well done, Lenny," said their father.

"What?" said Sadie.

"I think it's a lovely present that Len has brought," said Jack's father. Then he winced.

The man at the cupboards noticed the wincing. "Pie," he shouted into the snug. "Stop torturing that piano." The piano stopped for half a second, then started again with more deliberation.

"A work of art, really," said one of the sisters.

Sadie looked at Jack. He shook his head.

"A very honored wedding *guest*," said Fiona.

"Do fuh-*kawf*," said Jack, in one of the exaggerated English accents he sometimes slid into. He had dozens of them, similar but for subtly different uses, like the blades of a penknife. He added, "*Would* you."

"The lingering log of Len," said Jack's father.

Then the little boy was back, and said to Sadie, with the same jubilation, "It's a turd won't flush!" He set his hand on Sadie's knee. She had never been so glad for a human touch in her life.

The assembled Valerts laughed silently. It was a laugh Sadie recognized from Jack: to make noise would ruin the joke.

"It *is* tenacious," said Fiona. "It's quite a tenacious turd."

"Oh, that's right," Jack's father said to Sadie, as though noticing her for the first time. He regarded her with an intensity she couldn't interpret. Kindly? Aggressive? Flirtatious? "Americans don't appreciate the scatological, do they?"

"We do," said Sadie, thinking, *I don't.* The kitchen table was at an angle to the walls, and it gave her a headache. She could feel the sugar from the strawberry sandwich in her molars. How far was town? Could they get out of there? She looked up at Jack. "Coffee?"

"That's right, I was going to make some."

"This is my father," said Fiona. She squinted at the smoke from her cigarette. "Daddy, this is Sadie. I'm sorry you won't meet my mother."

"No?" said Sadie to Jack.

"She's unwell," said Michael Valert. "Rotten timing." It was his eyes that confused things, so joltingly blue they seemed to hold every emotion and its opposite. "You must be absolutely *shattered*," he told her.

"Not too bad."

"All that driving. I'd be shattered. I *am* shattered."

"S'shame," said Jack. "About Ma."

"Can't be helped," said Fiona. "We're videotaping it."

Jack set a cup of coffee on the table. The little plastic jug in front of her was marked MILK. "Cream?" she said to Jack.

He shook his head. "I'm going to help Piet set up the tables for the reception. You all right?"

She nodded. She understood that she would be, in some way, abandoned to these English people. "What can I do to help?" she asked the room at large.

"Nothing *to* do," said Fiona. She dropped her cigarette down the neck of a beer bottle on the counter, which was already filled with cigarettes. "The Dutch have it in hand."

"We're going for a walk, if you'd like to come," said Eloise.

"That sounds nice."

"You can borrow a pair of boots and a coat."

As Sadie passed Michael Valert, he said, "It's a large turd. Impressive. You must be feeding him well."

The boots wouldn't go over Sadie's thick calves, so she put on her wet shoes, a pair of rubber-soled Mary Janes. The coat wouldn't button over her hips, so she wore it open. By *we*, Eloise had meant herself and a small, wild-eyed, disheveled terrier who looked like the dog in the Arnolfini portrait and whose name was, apparently, Shithead. Sadie followed the two of them out the door, across a field, and then, dismayingly, up a hill.

"It's an amazing house," said Sadie, to prove to Eloise that she wasn't too out of breath to talk. "Why Ireland?"

"Why indeed. Apparently they like the Irish. I think they're mad to have bought it."

"Why?"

"It'll take them donkey's years to fix it up. Not to mention the cost. They're not very practical. Here, let's go this way." Eloise opened a gate that said BEWARE OF BULL. "Come on."

Sadie pointed at the sign and said, "Bull?"

Eloise's hat was large and tweed. It had fallen over her eyes; she knocked the brim up with her fist and scanned the field. "Look," she said. "He's over there. Come on! Don't be wet."

"I'm—they move fast, don't they?"

"He won't bother us. Come on, Shithead," she called in a sweet, threatening voice. "Shitty! *Shitty*."

The dog crossed first and they followed, and then climbed through some barbed wire, which caught in Sadie's hair. She could feel the wet shoes tugging at her tights, the waistband of which had fallen below the equator of her bottom. She slid in the mud. At the moment she thought Eloise was purposefully testing or torturing her, but eventually she would learn that this was simply every walk in the country with every English person she ever met: mud and injury and a disregard for safety or private property.

"What do you do?" she asked Eloise.

The hat was down again; she punched it up again. "Really? I'm a doctor. Len didn't tell you."

"Of course!" she said, though he hadn't. "I meant what kind of doctor."

"Nephrologist."

Sadie looked at her watch. "What time is the wedding?"

"Five."

"It's one."

"'Tis," said Eloise.

"Does Fiona need help? Getting ready? If your mother's not here."

"The Dutch will do that. They're very good, the Dutch. Why, are you tired? We can go back. Lenny's told me all about *you*."

"Oh," said Sadie. "Sorry your mother's not here."

"She's got gout."

"Really?"

"You think she'd lie?"

"No. I just—I guess I didn't realize women get gout."

"Runs in families," said Eloise, and Sadie realized there was nearly nothing Eloise did not deliver as a threat. "This way."

They seemed to be angling back down the hill. She thought it was a hill; it might have been a mountain. "Lucky it stopped raining."

"Ground'll be wet for the wedding."

"Are there roofs over the stables?"

"Yes," Eloise said. "But for the dancing there's not."

"There's dancing?"

"The Dutch will want to dance, surely," said Eloise. "And you. Americans are always dancing, aren't they? Shitty!" called Eloise, in a headmistress voice. "Shithead! Get over here." Then, carelessly, "I hope you weren't bothered."

"Oh, gosh, no," said Sadie. "By what?"

"My father. He has a childish sense of humor."

At the house they went in a door at the back, yet another one. Eloise bundled the dog in a dirty pink towel the color of a tongue, then tucked him under her arm. "Do you want a tour?"

"Sure."

"We'll take the back stairs."

Like servants do, thought Sadie, who'd read enough books about English girls in peril to wonder whether she was about to be shut in an attic.

Until recently the house had been owned and occupied by a single old man, who had died alone in one of the bedrooms. Somebody, perhaps the old man when he was a young man, had painted the walls with vivid tempera, which gave the rooms the intense look of Renaissance frescoes, brand-new, ancient, like marriage itself. The old man's bedroom was blue. *Lapis lazuli*, thought Sadie. Had his family died? His wife, his children? But the old man had never married: it had been his parents and brother and sisters who had died or disappeared, one at a time. That was family, too. No man who'd ever been married could have died thus: alone but perfectly happy in his bed, a portrait of the Virgin Mary hung at a tilt over his head so he didn't have to hurt his neck to look at her.

"Sad to die alone," said Sadie.

"How do *you* know?" asked Eloise. She set the dog on the ground. He sniffed at the threshold of the room but didn't go in. "I'm longing for it. But instead I will be surrounded by my children and grandchildren."

"Oh!" said Sadie. "You have children."

"Grown," said Eloise. "Elsewhere." Then, in an exaggerated English accent, though her own accent was already extremely English, "Gawn."

Sadie noticed her suitcase in the corner of the room, Jack's duffel next to it. The bags had been repacked, zipped up. She hoped it had been Jack who'd done it. She suspected it wasn't.

Half the rooms were derelict and half under construction and absolutely nothing was finished. There were sinks in odd places, unhinged doors leaning on walls. The floors were wood, dusty, any varnish worn away. Everything felt precarious but also beautiful, an excellent place, thought Sadie, for starting a life together.

"What did you get as a present?" Eloise asked.

Sadie was happy to say. It had been her idea. "A guest book," she said. They had ordered it from Smythson's. It was leather-bound with the name of the house—Currock House—stamped in gold on the cover.

"*What?*" said Eloise.

Sadie didn't know what misstep she'd made. Were you not supposed to say wedding presents before the wedding? But Eloise had asked!

"That's what I got," said Eloise. "You'll have to get something else."

"Well," said Sadie.

"Lottie's invited," said Eloise suddenly, as though the matter had been settled. "I'm sure Lenny said."

"The clown?"

At that Eloise laughed. It was a disconcerting laugh: you could see her tongue move with every peal, a rapid clapper in a bell. "Not a clown, no."

"Oh, that's right. Puppets. Right?"

"You don't know about Lottie! He *worshipped* her. But I'm *sure* he's told you."

He had mentioned Lottie—that she was older than he was, that they'd busked together on the streets of London. Not a girlfriend: just a woman. He'd been a teenager when they met. When Sadie thought of it, the act was in the jittery black and white of long ago. But he never spoke of worship. Her ankles were sore. She wondered if there was somewhere to take a nap, or even time enough.

"You must make him tell you about Lottie," said Eloise. "It's important."

"All right," said Sadie. She crouched to the dog. "Hello, Shithead."

"His name," said Eloise, "is *Seamus*."

"Oh! I thought—"

"Shithead's his nickname," said Eloise, fondly, to the dog.

The wedding was at five, with reception to follow. Most of the party went to the hotel in town to get ready, but the broke relatives—Sadie and Jack, Katie and Fred and their children—stayed behind. Sadie and Jack got ready in the blue bedroom, where the old man had died.

"Where's my bag?" said Jack. They had not been together long enough to pack in the same suitcase.

"There. Is your family always like that?"

"English? Yes."

"Obsessed with shit."

He laughed. "Right. *English*. That didn't bother you."

"I've had anxiety dreams more relaxing. Shame about your mother's gout."

"Gout? No gout. Where did you get gout?"

"Eloise said."

"Yes, she would. No: the problem is that Fiona converted to Catholicism and is now marrying an atheist."

"Which is worse?"

"Hard to tell."

"How's being Jewish?" she asked. "If she's against Catholics."

"You're not Jewish."

"I am Jewish. Are you in the wedding party?"

"No."

"What's with the suit?"

He was stepping into striped pants. "It's my morning suit. It's what you wear to weddings."

"You *own* that suit?"

"Yes," he said. Then, "Your *mother's* Jewish."

"Yes, my mother's Jewish, so I'm Jewish."

"Says who?"

"Jews the wide world over. Didn't you know that? Matrilineal, mate."

"Huh," he said. "Don't call me *mate*. No, I think she'd be fine with that. You didn't choose it, after all."

"But what if I did?"

"Sadie," said Jack.

"What about Lottie?"

"She wasn't Jewish."

"Did you know she was invited to the wedding?"

Jack smiled, but he also began to arrange his hair, his

major vanity, the dark curls that he wore swept off his fore-head. "No, she's not," he said.

"Eloise said she was."

He laughed with some relief. "Don't believe what Eloise says."

"She says you worshipped Lottie."

"Bollocks I did."

"I love it when you speak British. And you didn't sleep together."

"Not often."

Sadie laughed. Jack didn't.

"Not often," he said again.

"Near the start or near the end?"

He took his hands from his hair. "Right near the middle," he said.

When they drove up to the church they were already rushed. "Why does the car smell of wet dog?" he asked, and Sadie thought, *Was that today?* It seemed like weeks ago. She hadn't had a chance to tell him the story, which she knew would delight him; it had slipped her mind.

She parked the car.

"Remember the emergency brake," he told her.

"I always do," she said, though she'd forgotten.

Inside the church they were hustled up to a front pew by a Dutch person in a red denim blazer. Nobody had to ask bride's side or groom's: the English were the ones in floral prints and hats and morning suits, and the Dutch were the ones in long braids and primary colors. Sadie turned to see if she could pick out Lottie among the guests, but all she could see were hats, an armada of them.

The wedding, being a wedding, passed without incident.

Afterward, they had drinks in the check-floored foyer of the house, with plates of pâté and toast handed around. The tempera paint on the walls rubbed off on people's clothing. The twins' hands were blue. Shithead's port side was green. The guests who got too close to the yellow walls came away looking pollinated.

"My mother would hate this," said Jack. "Better she stayed at home."

"Do you *like* weddings?" said Sadie.

"No," he said. Then, "Lucky for us we're already married."

Sadie laughed ruefully.

"That drunk guy," said Jack. "From the bar. Our first date. Didn't he pronounce us man and wife?"

"I don't think he was credentialed."

"He might have been a ship captain. Do *you* like weddings?"

She thought about it. The answer was no, but she thought she might like marriage.

"I don't know," she said. "They're all right. No," she said. "No. I don't."

"I didn't think so."

She was crying then.

"Oh no!" he said, startled. "No! What's the matter?"

The matter was she felt, all of a sudden, the force of his family, and understood them as quicksand, and didn't know whether she should get herself out or try to rescue both of them. Eloise, the father, even darling Fiona, even Katie's twin sons, Thomas and Robin, with their Rod Stewart haircuts and old-man outfits that matched everyone in the family. She'd understood matching clothing—tracksuits, Disneyland sweatshirts, striped pajamas—as a particularly American insanity. She didn't like the international version any better.

"I'll ask you one of these days," he said, fond and irritated. "When I get some things straightened out."

She was astonished he understood so little.

After all the rain they had a beautiful night. The ground was muddy, but the stables were paved and covered and strung with fairy lights. There was no dancing—dancing was canceled, because it had been planned for the field and the field was muck. "Like the Somme," observed Michael Valert to Sadie, daring her to get the reference, which she did not. There was no seating plan, just long tables laid out. It had been a small wedding.

Eloise was weeping. She had seen the guest book that Jack and Sadie had bought.

"It's *nicer*," she said to her father.

"No, it's not, I'm sure it's not."

"It is!" she said. Then she was crying into his shoulder, and Fiona was there, too, and they were all comforting Eloise, whose grown gawn children hadn't come.

"It can be a different kind of guest book!" said Fiona. "Yours is lovely." She looked at Sadie. "They're both lovely!"

Michael Valert had to play MC at the dinner, because Piet's best man was a small shy Dutch woman named Kick who'd refused. Jack and Kick went off to smoke a cigarette, but Michael Valert didn't care: he assumed his position at the microphone, and offered a toast that referenced, among other things, the morning shit that hadn't flushed, a number of jokes about the Dutch, one about the French—it turned out that Eloise's long-ago divorced husband had been French—and an unarmed American, who Sadie realized, with surprise, was her. "To the bride and groom!" said Michael Valert. She was at a table with the unmarrying sisters and their families. The two blond twins played mumblety peg with a butter knife and their sweet blue hands.

"Which one's Pie?" Sadie asked.

"They both are," said Katie. "Easier that way."

Instead of a cake there were three Dutch cheeses in graduated sizes. Where *was* Jack? Michael Valert announced into the microphone, "The bride and groom will now cut the cheese."

Now, *that*, thought Sadie, was funny, and she burst into delighted laughter.

That was how she discovered that the euphemism was only American, and she the only American there. Jack was American, too, no matter how he denied it, but Jack was elsewhere. When Sadie realized that everyone in the stables was looking at her, she began to laugh harder. Her laughter was not silent. She could hear herself shriek.

"What *is* it," hissed Eloise, and Sadie could only manage to say, "It means f-f-*fart*." Across the stable, Michael Valert stared at her with his exceptionally blue eyes, as amplified as his voice had been, and for a moment she felt ashamed but then, as though her soul had been turned over with a spade, the shame turned to jubilation. She could have stood and sung, she thought, though she could not sing. Indeed the bride and groom had cut the cheese. Fiona's dress was scallion green and glorious. The Dutch had put too much gel in her hair.

That night they slept in the room of the dead man—"What if he died in this bed," asked Jack, and Sadie, brave for once, said, "People have died everywhere, you can hardly avoid it, come here," and tomorrow they would drive to the Dingle Peninsula, and she would think, over and over, *I am going to drive off this road and ruin everything*, but she never did, and she told him about the cat and dog, and explained to him that she'd thought his father had purposely made a funny joke—*the bride and groom will now cut the cheese!*—and they both laughed so hard she had to pull over to the side of the road, and when they recovered they drove out to Inch, where they were the only people on the beach, and so quickly and laughingly had sex, there on the damp sand, there was not a place in all of Ireland that wasn't damp, but what else do you do when you are all alone, and liberated?

For now, when he came back to the table, he found Sadie laughing so hard she couldn't speak, and all his family arranged around her. She was *crying* with laughter, and every time she tried to explain, she laughed harder, and his family looked more appalled. "What is it?" asked Jack, who felt suddenly the depths of his love for her, like Pavlov's dogs, all of them in love with Pavlov.

"Why is that woman laughing," Michael Valert said into the microphone.

"Tell her to stop!" said Eloise. "Make her stop!"

But he couldn't, and she couldn't either.

PROOF

What beach this was, Louis wasn't certain. Rock and sand,
a harbor town, and everywhere the sort of broken pottery
he'd combed for as a boy in the 1940s. Let his brothers fill
their pockets with sticks and shells, ordinary sea glass: he
knew how to look for the curved ridge on the underside of a
slice of saucer. Flip it over and find the blue flowers of Holland or China, a century ago or more. Once, on the beach
outside their summer cottage down the Cape, he had found
two entire clay pipes, eighteenth century, while his six older
brothers sharked and sealed and barked in the water; beyond them he could see, almost, the ghosts of the colonists
who had used the harbor as a dump, casting their broken
pottery out so he could find it in his own era and put it in
his own pockets. But this wasn't the Cape, or even Massachusetts. His brothers were mostly dead. That is, they were
all of them dead but in his head only mostly; they washed
up alive every now and then, and Louis would have to ask
himself: Is Phillip alive? Is Julius, Sidney?

Study the beach. Here, half-buried: a tiny terra-cotta cow with its head missing, otherwise intact, plaything for a child dead before the Industrial Revolution. The sea-worn bottom of a bottle that read EDINBU before the fracture. Lots of bits of plate, interesting glaze, violet and coppery brown. All his outgrown fixations had returned to him now that he was old. On an ordinary day in his bedroom at home he might hesitate to reach down for fear of falling over. Not here. He found the pottery and snatched it up. A teapot spout. A cocked handle from just where it had met cup. A round brown crockery seal with a crown and the word FIREPROOF. He thought: *that which is fireproof is also waterproof*, but he wasn't sure whether that were true. Good picking anyhow. Some boy was calling far off for his father, "Dad! Dad!" He looked up. He was that father. There was his boy. Boy: a full-grown man, shouldering a plaid bag, standing on the steps that led from the storefronts of the harbor town down to the little beach. On the street above a man in a kilt passed by. A Lady from Hell. What they called the Black Watch. They were in Scotland. His son had brought him here, to this island.

"We'll miss the boat," his son said.

"Let's not," Louis answered, and put the treasure in his pockets.

He had wanted a kilt and Arlene (née MacLean) had forbidden it: that was the story of their marriage. He was one of those Jews who could pass for a Scot, redheaded and black-humored. Why did he want a kilt so? He liked to sing:

Let the wind blow high, let the wind blow low.
Through the streets in my kilt I'll go.
All the lassies shout, Hello!
Donald, where's your troosers?

It had never been about the kilt, of course. He was the youngest of seven brothers, none of whom ever married, except him, at the age of forty-seven. Before that, and for years, he and his brothers had run the family department store in Montville, Massachusetts. Back then, their parents dead, the brothers went every year down the Cape for two weeks' vacation, crammed into a cottage called Beach Rose, until Arlene MacLean met Louis Levine in Wellfleet and took him away. He had deserted one family and only wanted to belong to the next. He'd thought he might wear a kilt to their wedding. "Oh no," said Arlene. "No kilt." "But your uncles—" "No kilts anywhere." "Bagpipes?" "I hate them." What could be sadder in a marriage than incompatible feelings about bagpipes? Ought they still marry? They eloped, and had a child, and never argued, except for the one thing. It became a running joke: the man wanted a kilt. "I have fine calves," he said. He immersed himself in everything Scottish: his favorite movie took place on the Isle of Mull, in the Inner Hebrides. "Look at that light," he would say to his family, who didn't care for the black-and-white light of the 1940s, not when modern times were right outside the door, and plenty well lit.

Now Arlene MacLean Levine was two months dead, and

his son had taken him to Scotland, to tour Mull, its castles and coastline, its birdlife: today they would take a boat to an uninhabited island that promised puffins. David himself didn't like birds, couldn't tell them apart, didn't want to: it struck him as feeble-minded, to stare at the throats and tails of birds for a flush or flash, just so you could name them. Seagull, pigeon, chicken, hawk, that was all you needed. All other birds were sparrows to him. As a child he'd found his father's ornithological obsession a moral failing: his father had never asked a single question about his son's life, or any other living human's. Louis loved animals, ate them; the mass grave of the local natural history museum had made David a vegetarian at age thirteen. *Study me*, he'd wanted to say to his father: the narrow-footed David, the bearded Levine, the flat-bottomed vegetarian. *Write me down in your book.*

He'd brought his father to Scotland, paid for everything, in attempt to ease the guilt he felt for living so far away, for having preferred distance all his adult life. He'd given his father birds and haggis and properly smoky, properly spelled whisky. A kilt, if it came to that.

He missed his gloomy mother. Together they called Louis the Infernal Optimist. He'd burn the house down looking for a bright side.

They boarded the boat in brilliant Tobermory. One of the men who worked for the tour company helped Louis down with a gentle hand. *Poor old Dad*, thought David. Then the man offered him the same courtly assistance. "Down you go," said the man, in the analgesic voice of a nurse. The boat was filled with the particular anxiety of paying customers who all wanted the best seat.

"Here, Dad," said David. He gestured to the bench along the gunwale.

David was not superstitious except in this way: he liked to feel lucky. No black cat or broken mirror bothered him, he never crossed fingers or made wishes, but every day was an omen for itself. He oscillated between his father's cheer and his mother's dolor: everything was perfect, unless it went to shit. The sun was shining in Scotland, clouds like storybook sheep above them though the local sheep were goatish, angular, weird. It was a good day, which meant it would be a good day, which meant every day for a while might be good. He'd packed the plaid picnic tote provided by the house they'd rented: bottle of water, bottle of wine, truckle of cheese, bread, cookies, fruit. They would picnic among the puffins.

Over the PA came the voice of the captain, the voice of God.

"Beautiful day," he said. "This is our one day of Scottish summer, and you're lucky to have it. Should be a nice trip to the Treshnish Isles, little more than an hour's journey. First stop is Lunga, where we'll have two hours, then to Staffa and Fingal's Cave. If you have any questions, Robby will answer."

Robby was the man who'd helped them into the boat. Now that he had a name, he became particular, a smiling man in oilskins, one starboard dimple, a boxer's nose. David tried to decide whether to dislike him.

"Finkel's Cave?" said Louis.

"Fingal's," said Robby.

"Finkel," said Louis.

Robby shook his head, smiling uncertainly. "Fingal. Guh-guh-guh. Scottish giant. Same hexagonal rock formation as the Giant's Causeway in Ireland. Basalt pillars."

David said to Louis, "Finkel's Cave sounds like one of your competitors."

Levine's of Montville had closed the year before David's birth; his father was already managing the benefits office of the hospital. The escalators, the layaway counter, the sliding oak and iron ladders in the storeroom, all gone, the Levine brothers dispersed, dead, buried in a line in the Jewish section of the Montville cemetery. Louis Levine, in the back of a boat headed to the uninhabited Treshnish Isles, was the last bit of equipment: a blinking man, a blinking sign, LEVINE'S, LEVINE'S, LEVINE'S.

All shipwrecks begin with a ship. David assessed the other passengers. Who would be saved and who lost? His father still went to the Y most mornings to swim laps, could save himself, but David was sturdy and without children and was certain that Robby would deputize him in case of catastrophe. He decided he would rise to the occasion.

A group of tall Swedes carried their lunches in waist packs and would not sit down, a hale septuagenarian English couple wore matching sensible shoes that looked like baked potatoes. The largest group came from some Eastern European country. It was hard to pick out how they were all related, easy to find their darling, a beautiful ten-year-old girl with Down syndrome. She had dark brown hair and prodigiously thick eyelashes, slate blue eyes, salmon cheeks. A selkie, a very selkie: at any moment she might assume her seal form and dive into the water. She scanned the horizon with binoculars and then, laughing, trained them on the faces of her family. David looked at his father, whose brother Sidney had had Down syndrome, too—Sidney, like all the brothers, had worked at the store until he died.

But Louis: Louis had forgotten where he was again. This was his secret. These days, when he daydreamed (dreamy Louis, all the time), he lost himself. His brain went along its track and when coming around did not recognize the station. Still, a station: you could make sense of it, you could navigate any train station in the world, despite the language, the local customs. Train stations obeyed. Keep tight till you know where you are, you'll be all right. Outside the boat, the water flashed, bent, bulged, and fish—fish! He said it to his son, "Fish!"

"Dolphins!" said David. "Look!"

Blue sky and dolphins, the wind battering their ears, a laughing girl, a picnic at their feet: a triumph.

"Will there definitely be puffins?" a tall Swedish woman asked.

"Were yesterday," said Robby.

"Is it guaranteed?"

"Puffins yesterday, most likely puffins today," Robby said. "Sir!"

Louis was leaning over the side of the boat, kneeling on the bench and staring at the water. The Swedish woman grabbed him by the collar of his coat. "*Upla*," she said, gentling Louis back on his seat.

"Hey," said Robby to David. "Look after your father."

"He's—"

"Look after him," said Robby.

"All right, folks," said the voice of God. "We're going to go take a closer look at our friends on that rock."

The rocks in a line on the larger rock lifted their heads and revealed themselves to be seals.

"Oh, the sweet things," said Louis, and the laughing girl gasped, went silent, laughed again. "Puffin," Louis said suddenly; he thrust his finger skyward at a flying bird— "Puffin, puffin."

"Puffin," the girl agreed.

"Puffins can't fly," said David.

"Yes, they can," said several voices in several accents.

"You're thinking of penguins," said Robby.

"I thought—"

"Puffins fly," said Robby firmly. Then he leaned in and said in David's ear, so the children couldn't hear, "Don't confuse them with penguins. They fuckin' hate that."

The website for the tour had said that the path to the puffins was rocky. What they meant was boulderous. Each rock was the size of a human head or larger, and loose, and shifted when you stepped. "Look for the flat ones!" called Robby, who would stay on the boat. People stood on their rocks, trying to figure out which way might not kill them. *Disaster*, thought David. He tried to keep the picnic bag on his back, but it kept swinging to his front and knocking him off balance. His mother might have been delighted by a fancy picnic; every morning for years his father had stuck a deviled ham sandwich in his back pocket and sat on it till lunchtime, when it was warm and flat and ready to eat. He needed, he had always needed, so little. David started crawling over the rocks on all fours, the bag a ringing bell of stupidity. His father was seventy-seven. They had no business here. The tour company should have warned him.

"Are you all right?" the Englishwoman called.

David straightened up to see his father standing like a statue on a rock, facing a little inlet. Marooned. He'd gone the wrong direction.

"Do you need a hand, Dad?"

No answer. His father could do this sometimes, get lost in thought, but in an armchair. What happened if an old man broke his hip on the Treshnish Isles? Would he be airlifted to safety? Buried at sea?

"Dad!" David shouted, then all around him, the voices of his fellow passengers like birdcall: "Sir!" "Sir!" "Hey!" "Buddy!" "My friend!" "Sir!"

Slowly, his father pivoted. He gave a fluttering wave with the back of his hand and made his way tightroperly across the rocks.

On the shore, they were confronted with a muddy path straight up a hill. David struggled with the bag. Ahead of him, Louis walked up at an angle, as though against the wind, dipping his fingertips in the mud. Then they stood on a wide green plateau. David turned and regarded the view: blue sky above, slate sea below, grass and—

—his father said, in a fond voice, "Oh, little brothers. Look, Davey, look at them."

White-breasted, orange-beaked, hopping along the ground, birds the size of books: puffins, dozens of them, so many you couldn't count, or see them as individuals; they constituted mere puffinosity. People walked right up and took pictures. They were not seagulls nor pigeons, who begged for food or stole it: they were merely the locals, accustomed to the seasonal influx of gawkers. Patient, accessible, aloof. They could fly but chose not to. David pulled out his phone. He almost laughed when the bird in front of him appeared on the screen.

"I didn't think they'd be so close," he said. "Why aren't they afraid?"

"Because their predators are," said Louis. This fact was a shard of pottery: it lay there; he snatched it up. "The puffins know that if humans are near, their predators won't be. They live in burrows. See them hopping in and out?"

"They're so *sweet*," said David wonderingly. He wanted to pick one up, dandle it on his knee. There was more island to scale—the voice of God had told them that the views from the top of Lunga were astonishing—but why risk it when they were here and already astonished? He set down the bag. The puffins were endearing and ridiculous, with expressions that suggested they thought the same of you, coming all this way to gawk at puffins. He pulled out the cheese in its black wax armor and held it in his palm like Yorick's skull.

"Is that your father?" said a passing Swede.

His father had walked to the edge of the plateau, to the sheer drop that overlooked the bouldered beach. He leaned over on one foot, windmill-limbed.

The day was lovely, till Dad fell off the cliff.

"Come back!" called David. His father had once been afraid of heights (one thing they had in common). Now he leaned farther out. David knew he should go retrieve him; he didn't think he could. "Dad!"

His father folded his limbs together and pointed behind David, to the island's peak. "Let's go up."

"Well, I think—"

But his father was already heading toward the upward path, and David had to follow. He slipped the cheese back in the bag and left everything behind.

The ground was mud-shifty. You had to use your whole body to ascend. How was Louis moving so quickly? It was not, David thought, that he was acrophobic. He had acrophobia by proxy, which was just as bad. He felt everyone else was about to fall off the mountain: the old English people, the Swedes, above all his father, who seemed to have been bitten by one of the cliff-walking sheep on the Isle of Mull. David cursed his worn-out running shoes. He could not see his father. He hoped that their shipmates—there were several different boatloads of tourists on the uninhabited island—would look after him. The path was narrow. The mud persisted. He tried to keep his father safe with the force of his mind.

When he got to the top, his father was absolutely fine, not even out of breath, and peering into a little grotto.

"Nesting cormorants," said Louis. "Look. Mother and chick."

The cormorants were waist-high, with elongated mechanical heads. They looked as though they could nip your hands off like shears. David backed away. Even as a teenager he had understood his father's love of birds as a kind of religious belief: so deep a longing to see a winged creature it could not be satiated by a single sighting, you had to keep going, you knew you would never reach perfection, you strove for it even so, red-throated, yellow-tailed, lesser, greater. David was like any child of a zealot: he could not compete; he would not be comforted.

The voice of God was right: the view was astonishing. Boggling. Better than the view below? Yes. *All right*, David told himself. The walk was worth it. The day was saved. He felt some rigging in his soul relax. He could use some water, but he'd left it below.

"Beautiful!" said Louis, looking at the cormorants.

"Let's go down," said David, though he was frightened at the thought. Down was always worse.

Years before, when they were young—not young people, but a young family—they had gone to Plimoth Plantation, where you went to look at so-called pilgrims in their habitat, actors refusing to acknowledge the modern world while they went about their duties. This incensed Arlene, as did nearly anything that involved grown-ups pretending: children's television, or playing charades. She and David narrowed their eyes at the phonies. What a despicable way to earn your living! But Louis had loved it. The pilgrims' calmness as they dipped their candles, ground their corn. They reminded him of the Levine brothers. There was always something to do, back in the long ago. His brothers had started to die almost the moment Louis had left the house: he had turned out to be a load-bearing wall.

It was a pleasure to be among the puffins, who reminded him of the pilgrims, who reminded him of his brothers.

"Lunch among the little brothers," said Louis, once they got back to their bag. He had not read about puffins in years. Everything was there. "What their Latin name means. *Fratercula*: little brother. Because they look like monks, I guess, in robes. Myself I think puffins are Jewish."

"Because of the beaks."

"Not only. I'm Jewish myself, you know. They're pelagic. They fish at sea."

"Of course." David opened the box of crackers, which turned out to be charcoal black, like dog biscuits. The picnic tote even had a cheese board and knife, as well as plastic champagne flutes, cutlery, and plates for four, unnecessary and now comic. He cut a wedge of cheddar. "The company of puffins," he said.

Louis said, regarding one, "Arlene's trying to get rid of me."

"What—"

"She'd deny it."

"Dad. She died."

"I know that," said Louis, irritated. "Nevertheless."

Yes. She was dead. That didn't change things. Arlene had not trusted him to live alone. "We have to plan for the future," she'd said. Who wanted to? Let the future itself do the planning. Louis thought of his brother Sidney, who sometimes bothered the customers by simply existing, his beaming smile, his joy over strangers. "Why don't you put him in a home?" people asked. "He could be with other people like him." What they meant was: *I am different from him and do not wish to be near. Why don't you get rid of him?*

Because *I* want him near. Because he *is* with people like him, his family. Oh, Louis had never really wanted to leave his brothers, enter the world of ordinary people, life with a woman and all her, what were they, *accoutrements*. His brothers would have looked after him forever.

"The feeling persists," said Louis.

"Dad."

"I've lost your name," Louis said gently.

"Daddy!" said David.

Louis realized he'd said the wrong thing. "Of course I haven't. Don't be *daft*," he said, as though he'd become the Scotsman he'd wanted to be.

"Why did you say that?" said David, aware of the anger in his own voice. He understood what was happening, in a way; he knew it was an occasion for sympathy, not fury, but the sympathy he had—inexhaustible!—was buried beneath a layer of fury, and he had to tunnel through, he had to scrabble to get at it. He had to go back in time to before his father had forgotten his name, when he was saying unforgivable things. "*Dad*," he said again.

"I didn't. David," he said. There it was.

Louis knew what year it was, and he could do nearly everything for himself, but thinking clearly when he was daydreaming was like standing while asleep—he could not do it. The puffins hopped in and out of burrows, as if into stockrooms. His confusion hung between them; they both understood they wouldn't speak of it. Not till they'd been home for some months, and even then, it would be cautious. *Dad, you've forgotten. Yes, I suppose I have.*

"You got up here!" said a woman. "Good for you."

They turned to look. It was the mother of the Eastern

European family. Her English was confusingly accentless: not American nor English nor Scottish. "I wore the wrong shoes," she said, lifting her foot to display a white sneaker half-browned with mud. "I didn't understand."

"No," said David.

"Still it's lovely. Puffin therapy," said the woman. "They call it so."

"I can understand that," said Louis. He turned to look at the puffins. "They're peaceful. They give you a sense of peace. Don't you think, David?"

Well, yes, David looked at them and he felt better and he resented them. The birds indeed had the curvilinear heads of his father's family. He could believe that they *thought* things, which he had never believed about birds. (Some people love animals for how alien they are—that was Louis—others for how like—that was David.) Already he had convinced himself that momentarily forgetting his name was something his father might have done any day of his life.

Little brothers. *Fraterculi*. His *mizpocah*. No brothers but puffins, no uncles but puffins, no cousins. He wanted to call his mother.

"It lifts your heart," his father said to the woman, who answered, "All nature does, no?"

"No," said David. He didn't want it to be *all nature*. He wanted it to be something you had to travel for, a fairy-tale journey: a boat, another boat, a treacherous approach, an unhappy revelation, a comic one.

"Perhaps," said Louis.

"Cormorants," said David. "They're not uplifting."

"They are!" said the woman. "When they fly—"

"I'm not interested in birds when they fly," said David. Then, to change the subject, "Where are you visiting from?"

"Tomorrow we fly ourselves. To Helsinki."

"That's home?" Louis asked.

"That's home."

"Ah," David said, "you're *Finnish*."

"Finnish," said Louis. "Like a fish."

"Just so," said the woman. "Ah, here are my people."

Here they came. They seemed to have multiplied during their time on the island, led by the girl, laughing. She saw Louis, and waved, then her mother, to whom she ran. She said something in Finnish, a language David did not understand and therefore found irksome.

He repacked the bag, the glasses, the cheese with one wedge cut out. He drank as much of the bottle of water as he could, to make the bag lighter. For a flashing moment he thought, *Maybe I'll just walk off the cliff*, then, *Maybe Dad will*—he didn't want either of these things; it was all disaster or triumph for him, as usual. *Why is life so easy for some people?* he wondered, as he had many times in his life, though this time he wanted an actual answer. He thought it might be something you could study for.

The whole boat understood now: the old American man was their ward till the end of the day. The scramble across the rocks was no easier on the way back except that the picnic bag was emptier and it seemed more likely they'd survive. The Finnish woman took one of Louis's hands and one of her teenage boys took the other, and the girl with the binoculars led them back. Robby stepped from the boat and pointed at good rocks to step to, as though coaching a game of chess. "There's a flat one, and there's another, and another."

David knew his mother had not wanted to get rid of his father. Life did. His father had never been able to tell the difference between the two.

"We're lucky with the weather!" the Englishwoman with the potato shoes said to Louis as they settled in the boat.

"Are you?" said Louis. "Good for you."

The woman gave a wry smile, then said to David, "Did you get to the top?"

"My son has a fear of heights," said Louis.

"Vertigo," said the woman's husband, pointing to himself. They both had white hair that showed the pink of their scalps beneath. "Just found out. Hell of a way to do it."

"You're all right," said the Englishwoman.

"I bloody well am not," he said.

Staffa was a monumental lump of rock with a green top, vertically ribbed around the middle like a midcentury juice glass: spectacular, hard to make sense of. The boat came round and showed the maw of Fingal's Cave, dark and glittering, accessible only by a narrow ledge with rope bannister. If you stepped wrong you would end up on the rock below. It looked like the first stop in the afterworld, the place you'd come to in order to get sorted.

"Oh no," said David.

"No," agreed the septuagenarian Englishman. "You know, a bloke died here a few years back."

Again Robby leaned in close to David, to menace or joke

man-to-man. "Just the one. German. Backed off a cliff snapping his camera."

"Shall we go together?" the Englishwoman said to Louis, then to David, "I'll take him," as though this was what happened all the time: the fainthearted, the stumble-footed stayed behind, and a swap was made. The brave must go with the brave. The chickenshit sat with the chickenshit. For a moment David felt a wave of relief—when his father dropped from a height, as he'd been trying to do all day, it wouldn't be his fault. *I didn't even see it happen*, he imagined saying.

"You'll be my husband," said the Englishwoman to Louis, taking his hand.

"I'll *what*?"

"No, no," said David. "I'll come."

"Well done," said Robby, in a voice of doom.

You walked the ledge on the side of a sheer cliff, till you walked around the corner, and there it was, Fingal's Cave, a cathedral half-built by fairy folk. The ledge sloped up. Rock face to your right, a drop down to rocks on the left. The walls were built of basalt columns like polygonal organ pipes, gorgeous and threatening. The cave echoed. Some people balked going in, acrophobes and claustrophobes, and turned back and stepped down onto the hard rock beach, also made of the hexagonal rock but sawed off, the kind of geometry you wouldn't be surprised to see under a microscope, startling when life-sized and out in the open.

The cave was a vast space with the sea sloshing in; the ledge itself was narrow for one-way traffic, never mind the necessary two: people sidled in and saw what they wanted then turned around and had to negotiate the oncomers, who froze against the walls with unease or skirted the edge and tried not to look down. Why would you do it? It was nearly slapstick, strangers fitting their bodies together (bottom to pelvis, bosom to Adam's apple), reeling their arms in the air. Gravity is hilarious, until it kills you. Another thing his father had brought him to, full of excitement, that he had hated: silent movies at the revival house. Plimoth Plantation. The Museum of Natural History. The old battleship in the harbor. The graveyard to do rubbings. The trolley museum. His mother's wake.

"This is intolerable," David said aloud.

The Englishwoman reached behind with her free hand and took his.

Echoey commotion ahead. You couldn't come out unchanged. They should turn back. It was him. He was the weak one. The Finns were deep in. The mother with her muddy shoes looked less brave here, perhaps why she hadn't gone up the mountain on Lunga, and the daughter with Down syndrome was making little *ah-ah-ah* noises of care, and so she could listen to her voice echo. David thought he might faint. He tried to get his hand loose. If he did faint, if he did tip over, he would pull the Englishwoman down, and then his father, who might have joined up to who-knows-who in front. A daisy chain of tourists down, not just one careless German. Lunch for Fingal.

The story of this trip was supposed to be the past: Arlene was dead. He had thought the future was a ways away. *She would have hated to outlive me*, Louis had told David. The sad thing was she'd been looking forward to it. She loved him, she'd miss him: at least the house would be quiet.

All of a sudden, without planning to, David was sitting down.

"Op!" said somebody behind him.

He crossed his legs and leaned against the wall. Below him the water sloshed. Where did the tide go, when it went out? He always imagined it balling up in the middle of the ocean, but what if it were a blanket tugged between sleepers, first one side of the bed, then the other?

"Vertigo," he heard a woman pronounce in an English accent.

On either side of him people were trying to coax him to his feet. It was too narrow a foothold for kindness. Somebody tried to go behind him; another stepped over his legs.

"Get up," the Englishwoman said.

No. He would have to be pulled from the cave like a tooth. The only solution for fear was stubbornness. His mother had taught him that. She had raised him to believe in the power of obstinacy, and now, on an uninhabited island in a cathedral built by nobody, he clung to his faith. He was the only child of an old man. That had meant one thing when he was a boy, and meant new things now.

Then his father was there, leaning over, hands on thighs.

"Well," said Louis. "What have we here?"

"I should get up," admitted David.

Louis looked around them. On one side, a girl wearing binoculars regarded them. A bird-watcher, perhaps—those were good bird-watching glasses—and then Louis recognized her as one of Sidney's countrywomen, her face round and flat and, at the moment, impressed at this peculiar behavior. He sat down.

"This is not progress!" yelled one of the Swedes.

"Come on, friend," said Louis. "Let's stand up."

"I'm not your *friend*," said David.

Louis nodded. No, his beautiful, pessimistic son— pessimism is a form of cowardice, but Louis knew better than to say so to his beloved pessimists. "Nevertheless."

"I don't know how."

"The usual way, I think," said Louis. Then, helped by a dozen hands, as in a child's séance, they were lifted up, and the cave was filled with applause, genuine, sarcastic, dutiful.

Nobody mentioned anything on the boat home. "Subdued!" said Robby, appraising them as they boarded, one by one, then, to David, "You caught the Scottish sun. Rare but deadly. Should have worn a hat."

Back in Tobermory they passed a poster for the Highland Games, held that day at the golf course. Already the cabers were being packed up. *That's what we should have done*, David thought. By next month his father might not even remember the puffins. But around the world a story would be told, in Helsinki, in Devon, in Malmö: *A man panicked. We saved him. Without us he would have died.*

He would have to rearrange both their lives before the

worst happened. But not yet. Together they would fly back to Boston. David would go on to Seattle; from a distance he could pretend his father was fine. *It's not an emergency*, he told himself, though he knew otherwise, an emergency the way all of life was.

In front of the bank a teenage boy played violin for money; when David concentrated he recognized it as "Good Vibrations," heart-lifting and strange. He put his hands in his pockets and found one fifty-pence piece, polygonal like the rocks of Staffa. He tossed it into the open violin case.

"Got any pound coins?" David asked, and his father dug in his pockets, produced two handfuls of broken things.

That morning they'd been to the little history museum. Had his father stolen something? Blue, brown, violet: the pottery looked old, older than his father, than Levine's of Montville. Exhibition old. It was beautiful, timeworn, a jumble. These things had been broken for generations. David could not make sense of any of it.

"Where'd you get this?" He picked up the headless figure of a cow.

"There." Louis pointed at the beach. Low tide now, better picking.

"What are you talking about?"

His father gazed upon him with those pale eyes, gone mother-of-pearl with age. He pointed again. *"There."*

The two of them went down the concrete steps, greened from the tides. "Careful," said David. "Careful," said Louis. He leaned over, discovered a bit of teapot, with a black-and-white pattern that looked like a castle turret. He pointed to the ground, and David picked up a rhomboid piece of plate painted with radiating lashes of blue. A triangle of yellow plate with dark green flowers. A spout.

"Where did it come from?" said David.

"It washes up," said Louis. "The past. They used the harbor as a dump. Same as when I was a kid. There's a box of it, in the attic. That will come to you, too."

It would all come to David. They both knew it and hated it, and yet: saucer, lip, hand-painted flower. The tide went out, revealing things. The ocean would not swallow them today.

"Why didn't you *tell* me?" David said.

"I don't know," said Louis, but he remembered how little they ever agreed on.

They picked and picked, but they could not pick it all. Mere men could never undo the work of mere men. From the hill the sound of pipers: the games had ended; the pipers were headed squallingly home. The violinist quit; it wasn't a fair fight. David stood up, looked at the pieces on his palm, turned them all bright side up. A glory, so vivid and so unmendable. His now. The pipers blared louder. When he looked out toward the water he almost thought he could see them, the old people, the auld ones, casting their pottery into the sea just so he, David, David Levine, could find it generations later.

As for Louis, he had turned to the main street to watch the band of pipers round the corner onto Tobermory's main street. Dozens marching in time. So young, the pipers, high school kids, boys and girls—it was a girl in the front, spinning the red bass drumsticks. You could hear your own name in the music of the pipes, the names of all your ancestors and descendants, wherever they came from, wherever they were headed. What could be sadder than not loving this sound? Everything swung in time. He was alone on a beach as usual, gladdened, slaked, exhausted. The muscles of his legs twitched.

Oh, Arlene: it was always about the kilt.

IT'S NOT YOU

Hotels were different in those days. You could smoke in them. The rooms had bathtubs, where you could also smoke. You didn't need a credit card or identification, though you might be made to sign the register, so later the private detective— just like that, we're in a black-and-white movie, though I speak only of the long-ago days of 1993—could track you down. Maybe you anticipated the private detective, and wrote down an assumed name.

Nobody was looking for me. I didn't use an assumed name, though I wasn't myself. I'd had my heart broken, or so I thought; I had been shattered in a collision with a man, or so I thought; and I went to the fabled pink hotel just outside the midwestern town where I lived. The Narcissus Hotel: it sat on the edge of a lake and admired its own reflection. Behind, an ersatz lake, an amoebic swimming pool, now drained, empty lounge chairs all around. January 1: cold, but not yet debilitating. In my suitcase I'd brought one change of cloth-ing, a cosmetic bag, a bottle of Jim Beam, a plastic sack of

Granny Smith apples. I thought this was all I needed. My plan was to drink bourbon and take baths and feel sorry for myself. Paint my toenails, maybe. Shave my legs. My apartment had only a small fiberglass shower I had to fit myself into, as though it were a science fiction pod that transported me to nowhere, but cleaner.

I would watch television, too. In those days, I didn't own one, and there is a certain level of weeping that can only be achieved while watching TV, self-excoriating, with a distant laugh track. I wanted to demolish myself, but I intended on surviving the demolition.

It wasn't the collision that had hurt me. It was that the other party, who'd apologized and explained a catalog of deficiencies—self-loathing, an unsuitability for any kind of extended human contact—had three weeks later fallen spectacularly and visibly in love with a woman and they could be seen—seen by me—necking in the public spaces of the small town. The coffee shop, the bar, before the movie started at the movie theater. I was young then—we all were—but not so young that public necking was an ordinary thing to do. We weren't teenagers but grown-ups: late twenties in my case, early thirties in theirs.

New Year's Day in the Narcissus Hotel. The lobby was filled with departing hangovers and their owners. Paper hats fell with hollow pops to the ground. Everyone winced. You couldn't tell whose grip had failed. Nothing looked auspicious. That was good. My New Year's resolution was to feel as bad as I could as fast as I could in highfalutin privacy, then leave the tatters of my sadness behind, with the empty bottle and six apple cores.

"How long will you be with us?" asked the spoon-faced redheaded woman behind the desk. She wore a brass name tag that read EILEEN.

"It will only seem like forever," I promised. "One night."

She handed me a brass key on a brass fob. Hotels had keys, in those days.

I had packed the bottle of bourbon, the apples, my cosmetic bag, but had forgotten a nightgown. Who was looking? I built my drunkenness like a fire, patiently, enough space so it might blaze.

You shall know a rich man by his shirt, and so I did. Breakfast time in the breakfast room. The décor was old but kept up. Space-age, with stiff sputnikoid chandeliers. Dark pink leather banquettes, rosy pink carpets. Preposterous but wonderful. I'd eaten there in the past: they had a dessert cart, upon which they wheeled examples of their desserts to your table: a slice of cake, a crème brûlée, a flat apple tart that looked like a mademoiselle's hat.

I had my own hangover now, not terrible, a wobbling threat that might yet be kept at bay. I had taken three baths; my toenails were vampy red. I had watched television till the end of broadcast hours, which was a thing that happened then: footage of the American flag waving in the breeze, then here be monsters. In my other life, the one that happened outside of the Narcissus Hotel, I worked in the HR department of a radio station. I lived with voices overhead. That was why I didn't have a television. It would have been disloyal. I'd found a rerun on a VHF station of squabbling siblings and had proceeded to weep for hours, in the tub, on one double bed, then the other. Even at the time I knew I wasn't weeping over anything actual that I'd lost, but because I'd wanted love and did not deserve it. My soul was deformed. It couldn't bear weight.

The rich man sat at the back of the breakfast room in one of the large horseshoe booths built for public canoodling. His pale green shirt, starched, flawless, seemed to have been not ironed but forged, his mustache tended by money and a specialist. His glasses might have cost a lot, but twenty years before. In his fifties, I thought. In those days *fifties* was the age I assigned people undeniably older than me. I never looked at anyone and guessed they were in their forties. You were a teenager, or my age, or middle-aged, or old.

The waiter went to the man's table and murmured. The man answered. At faces I am no good but I always recognize a voice.

"Dr. Benjamin," I said, once the waiter had left. He looked disappointed, with an expression that said, *Here, of all places.* He inclined his head to recognize my recognition. "I listen to you," I told him.

He hosted an overnight advice show, eleven p.m. to two a.m., on another AM channel, not mine. He had a beef bourguignon voice and regular callers. Stewart from Omaha. Allison from Asbury Park, New Jersey. Linda from Chattanooga.

"Thank you," he said. Then added, "If that's the appropriate response."

"I'm in radio, too," I said. "Not talent. HR."

The waiter stood by my table, a tall young man with an

old-fashioned Cesar Romero mustache. When I looked at him he smiled and revealed a full set of metal braces.

"I will have the fruit plate," I said. Then, as though it meant nothing to me, an afterthought, "and a Bloody Mary."

It is the fear of judgment that keeps me behaving, most of the time, like the religious. Not of God but of strangers.

"Hair of the dog," the radio shrink said to me.

"Hair of the werewolf," I answered.

"You could be. On air. You have a lovely voice."

In my head I kept a little box of compliments I'd heard more than once: I had nice hair (wavy, strawberry blond), and nice skin, and a lovely voice. I didn't believe the compliments, particularly at such times in my life, but I liked to keep them for review, as my mother reviewed the scrapbooks from her childhood in a small town, when her every unusual move—going to England on a trip, performing in a play in the next town over—made the local paper.

Who in this story do I love? Nobody. Myself, a little. Oh, the waiter, with his diacritical mustache above his armored teeth. I love the waiter. I always love the waiter.

The Bloody Mary had some spice in it that sent a tickle through my palate into my nose. A prickle, a yearning, an itch: a gathering sneezish sensation. One in ten Bloody Marys did this to me. I always forgot. I took another drink and the feeling intensified. Beneath the pressure of the spice was a layer of leftover intoxication that the vodka perked up. I thought, not for the first time, that I had a sixth sense and it was called drunkenness.

"No good?" the radio shrink asked me.

"What?"

"You're making a terrible face."

"It's good," I said, but the sensation was more complicated than that. "What are you doing in this neck of the woods?"

"Is it a *neck*?" He touched his own neck with the tips of his fingers. "I like the rooms here."

"You probably have a nicer room than I do. The presidential suite. The honeymoon."

"I'm neither the president nor a honeymooner."

"Those're the only suites I know," I said. It was possible to be somebody else in a hotel; I was slipping into a stranger's way of speaking. I said, "Far from Chicago."

"Far from Chicago," he agreed. He picked up his coffee cup in both hands, as though it were a precious thing, though it was thick china, the kind you'd have to hurl at a wall to break. "Business," he said at last. "You?"

"I live here."

"You live in the hotel?"

"In town."

"Oh, you're merely breakfasting, not staying."

"I'm staying." I started to long for a second Bloody Mary as though for an old friend who might rescue me from the conversation. "Somebody was mean to me," I said to the radio shrink. "I decided to be kind to myself."

He palmed the cup and drank from it then settled it back

in the saucer. The green shirt was a sickening color against the pink leather. "It's a good hotel for heartbreak. Join me," he said, in his commercial break voice, deeply intimate, meant for thousands, maybe millions, of people.

There were other radio hosts in those days, also called doctors, who would yell at you. A woman who said to heartbroken husbands, *You better straighten up and fly right*. A testy man— *No, no, no, no: listener*—he called his listeners *listener— listener, this is your wake-up call.*

But Dr. Benjamin practiced compassion, with that deep voice and his big feelings. Once you forgive yourself, you can forgive your mother, he would say. Or perhaps it was the other way around: your mother first, then you. He told stories of his own terrible decisions. Unlike some voices, his had ballast and breadth. For some reason I had pictured him as bald, in a bow tie. I pictured all male radio hosts as bald and bow tied, until presented with evidence to the contrary. Instead he had a thatch of silver hair. The expensive shirt. Cowboy boots.

I listened to his show all the time, because I hated him. I thought he gave terrible advice. He believed in God and tried to convince other people to do likewise. Sheila from Hoboken, Ann from Nashville, Patrick from Daly City. On the radio it didn't matter where you lived, small town or the suburbs or New York City (though nobody from New York City ever called Dr. Benjamin): you had the same access to the phone lines and radio waves. You were allowed to broadcast your loneliness to the world, in the hours between eleven p.m. through two a.m. Central Standard Time. Every so often a caller started to say something that promised absolute humiliation and I would have to fly across the room to snap the radio off. *My husband cannot satisfy me, Doc—*

So long ago! I can't remember faces but I can remember voices. I can't remember smells but I remember in all its dimensions the way I felt in those days. The worst thing about not being loved, I thought then, was how vivid I was to myself.

Now I am loved and in black and white.

Up close he seemed vast. Paul Bunyan-y, as though he'd drunk up the contents of that swimming pool to quench his thirst, though he didn't look quenched. Those outdated glasses had just a tinge of purple to the lenses. Impossible to tell whether this was fashion or prescription, something to protect his eyes. His retinas, I told myself. He was all the way at the bottom of the hoop of the horseshoe, his body at an angle. I sat at the edge of the booth to give him room.

He said, "Better?"

"Maybe," I said. "Are you a real doctor?"

He stretched then, the tomcat, his arms over his head. His big steel watch slipped down his wrist. "Sure."

"You're not."

"I'm not a medical doctor," he allowed.

"I know that," I said.

"Then yes. Yes, I'm a doctor."

The table had an air of vacancy: he'd eaten his breakfast, and it had been tidied away except for the vest pocket bottles of ketchup and Tabasco sauce, and a basket filled with tiny muffins. I took one, blueberry, and held it to the light. The waiter delivered the second Bloody Mary I hadn't ordered, unless by telepathy. "You have a PhD," I said.

"Yes."

"It's strange."

"That I have a PhD?"

"That we call people who study English literature for too long the same thing we call people who perform brain surgery."

"Oh *dear*," he said. "Psychology, not English literature."

"I'd like to see your suite."

He shook his head.

"Why not?"

"I'm married," he said. "You know that."

I did. Her name was Evaline. He mentioned her all the time: he called her *Evaline Benjamin, the Love of My Life*.

"That's not what I mean," I said, and I tore the little muffin in half, because maybe it *was* what I meant. *No*, I told myself. Every time I walked down a hotel hallway I peered into open doors. Was there a better room behind *this* door? A better view out the window of the room? Out of all these dozens of rooms, where would I be happiest, by which I mean, least like myself? I only wanted to see all the hotel rooms of the world, all the other places I might be. I was waiting to be diagnosed.

He said, "You're a nice young woman, but you won't cut

yourself a break. All right," he said. "Okay. We can go to my suite. They've probably finished making it up."

Even the hallways were pink and red, the gore and frill of a Victorian valentine: one of those mysterious valentines, with a pretty girl holding a guitar-sized fish. The suite was less garish, less whorehouse, less rubescent, with a crystal chandelier, that timeless symbol of One's Money's Worth. The two sofas were as blue and buttoned as honor guards. A mint-green stuffed rabbit sat in a pale salmon armchair.

"What's that?" I asked.

He looked at it as though it were a girl who'd snuck into his room and had taken all her clothes off and here came the question: throw her out, or . . . not.

"A present," he said.

"Who from?"

"Not from. For. Somebody else. Somebody who failed to show up."

"A child."

He shook his big head. "Not a child. She must have lost her nerve. She was supposed to be here yesterday."

"Maybe she realized you were the kind of man who'd give a stuffed bunny to a grown woman."

He regarded me through the purple glasses. Amethyst, I thought. My birthstone. Soon I would be twenty-eight. "You are young to be so unkind," he observed. "She collects stuffed animals." He turned again to the rabbit and seemed to lose heart. "This is supposed to be a good one."

"What makes a good one?"

"Collectible. But also it's pleasant." He plucked it from the chair and hugged it. "Pleasant to hug."

"Careful. It's probably worth more uncuddled." I put myself on the chair where the rabbit had been. I don't know why I thought the chair might be warm. He sat in one of the corners of the sofa closest to me.

"I thought you might be her," he told me. "But you're not old enough. How old are you?"

"Twenty-seven."

"Not nearly old enough."

"Do I look like her?"

"Oh. I mean, I'm not sure." He made the rabbit look out the window, and so I looked, too, but the sheers were closed and all I perceived was light.

"A listener," I said. "A caller. You're meeting somebody. Linda from Chattanooga!"

"Not *Linda* from *Chattanooga*," he said contemptuously. He put the rabbit next to him, as though aware of how silly he had looked. After a while he said, "Dawn from Baton Rouge."

I couldn't remember Dawn from Baton Rouge. "What does she look like?"

"I only know what she tells me."

"Should've asked for a picture."

He shrugged. "But: cold feet. So it doesn't matter."

"And now you've invited me instead," I said, and crossed my legs.

"Oh God, no," he said. "No, darling—"

I was aware then of what I was wearing: a pair of old blue jeans but good ones, a thin black sweater that showed my black bra beneath. Alluring, maybe, to the right demographic, slovenly to the wrong one.

"Sweetheart," he said. He got up from the sofa. It was a complicated job, hands to knees and a careful raising of the whole impressive structure of him. "No, let's have a drink." He went to the minibar, which was hidden in a cherry cabinet and had already been unlocked, already been plundered, already been refreshed. Imagine a life in which you could approach a minibar with no trepidation or guilt whatsoever.

He lifted a midget bottle of vodka and a pygmy can of Bloody Mary mix; he didn't know I'd only ordered a Bloody Mary because it was acceptable to do so before ten a.m. He was a man who drank and ate what he wanted at any time of day.

"We'll toast to our betrayers," he said.

Because it was something he might say to a midnight caller, I said, "I thought we only ever betrayed ourselves."

"Sometimes we look for accomplices. No ice," he said, turning to me. "To get through this we're gonna need some ice."

For a moment it felt as though we were in a jail instead of a reasonably nice hotel, sentenced to live out our days—*live out our days* being another way to say *hurtle toward death*.

In those days it was easy to disappear from view. All the people who caused you pain: you might never know what happened to them, unless they were famous, as the radio shrink was, and so I did know, it happened soon afterward, before the snow had melted. He died of a heart attack at another hotel, and Evaline Benjamin, the Love of His Life, flew from Chicago to be with him, and a guest host took over until the guest host was the actual host and it slid from a call-in advice show to a show about unexplained phenomena: UFOs. Bigfoot. I suppose it had been about the unexplained all along. All the best advice is on the internet now anyhow. That person who broke my heart might be a priest by now, or happily gay, or finally living openly as a woman, or married twenty-five years, or all of these things at once, or 65 percent of them, as is possible now in our world. It's good that it's possible. A common name plus my bad memory for faces: I wouldn't know how to start looking or when to stop.

The minibar wasn't equal to our thirsts. He sat so long, staring out the window, that I wondered whether something had gone wrong. A stroke. The start of ossification. Then in a spasm of fussiness he untucked his shirt.

He said, "In another life—"

"Yeah?"

"I would have been a better man. How long?"

"How long what?"

"Was your relationship with whoever broke your heart."

"He didn't break my heart."

"'Was mean to you,'" he said, with a playacting look on his face.

I did the math in my head, and rounded up. "A month."

"You," he said, in his own voice, which I understood I was hearing for the first time, "have got to be fucking kidding me."

It had actually been two and a half weeks. "Don't say I'm young," I told him.

"I wouldn't," he said. "But someday something terrible will happen to you and you'll hate this version of yourself."

"I don't plan on coming in versions."

"Jesus, you *are* young." Then his voice shifted back to its radio frequency, a fancy chocolate in its little matching rustling crenellated wrapper. "How mean was he?"

"He was nice, right up until the moment he wasn't."

"Well," he said, "so. You're making progress. Wish him well."

"I wish him well but not *that* well."

But that wasn't true. I wanted them both dead.

"The only way forward is to wish peace for those who have wronged you. Otherwise it eats you up."

I wished him peace when I thought he was doomed.

How can it be that I felt like this, over so little? It was as though I'd rubbed two sticks together and they'd detonated in my lap.

"I bet you have a nice bathtub," I said.

"You should go look."

I got myself a dollhouse bottle of bourbon. At some point he'd had ice delivered, in a silver bucket, with tongs. I had never used ice tongs before. I have never used them since. The serrations bit into the ice, one, two, five cubes, and I poured the bourbon over, a paltry amount that didn't make its way to the bottom of the glass, it just clung to the ice, so I got another. The bathroom was marble—marble, crystal,

velvet, it would be some years before hotels stopped model-
ing opulence on Versailles. There was a phone on the wall
by the toilet. I ran myself a bath and got in. This was what
I needed, not advice or contradiction, not the return of the
person who broke my heart, because I would not be able to
trust any love that might have been offered. It took me a long
time, years, to trust anyone's.

The door opened, and another miniature bottle of whis-
key came spinning across the floor.

"Irish is what's left," said the radio shrink through the
crack of the door.

"You're a good man," I said. "You are one. If you're worried that you're not."

Then he came in. He was wearing his cowboy boots and
slid a little on the marble. Now he looked entirely undone.
In another version of this story I'd be made modest by a
little cocktail dress of bubbles, but no person who really
loves baths loves bubble baths, nobody over seven, because
bubbles are a form of protection. They keep you below the
surface. They hide you from your own view. He looked at
me in his bathtub with that same disappointed look: just like
you to bathe in your birthday suit.

"I have some advice for you," I said to him.

"Lay it on me," he said.

"*Lay it on me.* How old are you?"

He shook his head. "What's your advice?"

"You should call your callers *Caller*. Like, *Are you there,
Caller?*"

"They like to be called by name."

"Overly familiar," I said.

"That's your advice."

"Yes," I said.

He was sitting on the edge of the tub then. The ice in his glass, if there had ever been any, had melted. I had no idea what he might do. Kiss me. Put a hand in the water. His eyebrows had peaks. Up close his mustache was even more impressive. I had never kissed a man with a mustache. I still haven't. It's not that I'm not attracted to men with mustaches but that men with mustaches aren't attracted to me.

"Can I have your maraschino cherry?" I asked.

"No maraschino cherry."

"I love maraschino cherries. All kinds. Sundae kinds, drink kinds, fruit cocktail. Tell me to change my life," I said to him, and put a damp hand on his knee.

"I won't tell you that."

"But I *need* someone to tell me."

He put his glass down where the little bottle of shampoo was. Such a big hotel. So many minuscule bottles. "You must change your life," he said.

"Good but I'm going to need some details."

"I keep sitting here I'm going to fall into the water." He stood up. "You know where to find me."

There isn't a moral to the story. Neither of us is in the right. Nothing was resolved. Decades later it still bothers me.

No way to tell how much later I awoke, facedown in the bath, and came up gasping. I had fallen asleep or I'd blacked out.

It was as though the water itself had woken me up, not the water on the surface of me, which wasn't enough, not even the water over my face like a hotel pillow, up my nose, in my lungs, but the water that soaked through my bodily tissues, running along fissures and ruining the texture of things, till it finally reached my heart and all my autonomic systems said, *Enough, you're awake now, you're alive, get out.*

That was one of the few times in my life I might have died and knew it. I fell asleep in a bathtub at twenty-seven. I was dragged out to sea as a small child; I spun on an icy road into a break in oncoming traffic on Route 1 north of Rockland, Maine, and miraculously stayed out of the ditch; I did not have breast cancer at twenty-nine, when it was explained to me that it was highly unlikely I would, but if I did, it was unlikely, it would be fatal, almost never at your age, but when at your age, rapid and deadly.

Those are the fake times I almost died. The real ones, neither you nor I ever know about.

The radio shrink would have said, *I guess she died of a broken heart*, and I would have ended my life and ruined his, for no reason, just a naked drunk dead woman in his room who'd gotten herself naked, and drunk, and dead.

But I wouldn't see the radio shrink again. I was gasping and out of the tub, and somebody was knocking on the bathroom door. I don't know why knocking—the door was unlocked—but the water was sloshing onto the floor, the tap was on, it couldn't have been on all this time, and I would find out it was raining into the bathroom below, I had caused *weather*, and the radio shrink had packed up and left but had hung the DO NOT DISTURB sign on his door, and had paid

for my room. Was gone. Dawn from Baton Rouge was a dis-
embodied voice again, but the redheaded woman from the
front desk, Eileen, she was here, slipping across the floor,
tossing me a robe, turning off the tap, tidying up my life.

"You're all right," she said. I could feel her name tag
against my cheek. "You should be ashamed of yourself, but
you're all right now."

I would like to say this was when my life changed. No. That
came pretty quick, within hours, but not yet. I would like to
say that the suggestion of kindness took. That I went home
and wished everyone well. That I forgave myself and it was
as though my fury at myself was the curse: forgiveness trans-
formed me and I became lovely. All that came later, if at all.
He was wrong, the shrink: nothing ever happened to me that
made me cry more than I did in those weeks of aftermath.
I'm one of the lucky ones. I know that. I became kinder the
way anybody does, because it costs less and is, nine times
out of ten, more effective.

At some point it had snowed. Last night, this morning. It
had been hours since I'd been outside. The snow was still
white, still falling, the roads with the ruts of tires. Soon the
snowplows would be out, scraping down to the pavement.
My clothing, left behind by the side of the tub, had gotten
sopping wet, so I was wearing a sweat suit abandoned by
some other guest at the Narcissus Hotel, found by Eileen, a
stranger's socks, too, my own shoes and winter coat. I had

to walk past the house of the couple who'd been necking everywhere, a story that seemed already in the past. By *past* I mean I regretted it, I was telling the story in my head. The woman I hadn't been left for drove a little red Honda. There it sat in her driveway, draped in snow. That was all right. It was a common car in those days, and I saw it and its doppelgangers everywhere. Even now a little red Honda seems to have a message for me, though they look nothing like they used to. *When will this be over,* I wondered as I walked in the snow. The humiliation is what I meant. Everything else is over, and all that's left is the vehicle of my humiliation.

You would recognize my voice, too. People do, in the grocery store, the airport, over the phone when I call to complain about my gas bill. Your voice, they say, are you—?

I have one of those voices, I always say. I don't mind if they recognize me but I'm not going to help them do it.

He kept telling me I had to be kind. Why? Why on earth? When life itself was not.

A SPLINTER

When Lenny was sixteen he ran away from home. Sailed. Bussed, as in bussing tables. Walked, from table to table to the ship's kitchen and back, round and round the decks of the *Queen Elizabeth 2*, on its voyage from New York to Southampton. His family knew he'd gone—his father had helped him land the job—they just expected him to turn around with the boat itself, same job, opposite direction, home in two weeks. But instead of spending a single day wandering Southampton he hitchhiked to London and tried to get a job in show business. "How *stupid*," his mother said, when she heard the news. She was English. He was not. Or he was, but in a way that only he understood.

He had gone to London because he'd fallen in love with a lady ventriloquist on board the ship. If he could have smuggled himself off in her trunks he would have, but she already had a man packed away. A toy man: his name was Willie Shavers. She also had a parrot, a little girl with braids, and a yellow cat. It was the parrot she was famous for: the parrot's name was Squawkanna, and with Lottie—Lottie was the woman, Lottie Stanley—she'd had a hit song, though that had been ten years before, in the mid-1970s. Famous for a summer. If you heard her name and were English, you'd say, *Who?* and if you heard the song you'd say, *Oh, right.* You might wince. It wasn't a good song. On board the *QE2*, Lenny had watched Lottie's act every single night. She was plump in her sequined gowns, and wore her blond hair in an old-fashioned hairdo, with lots of hair spray and a series of paste tiaras. She'd given him her calling card with a flourish, amused by his attention, and now here he was, ringing her bell at the address in Ladbroke Grove, being shown in by the doorman and sent down the hallway to her ground-floor flat.

The hairdo had been a wig, the glamorous face largely makeup, the cheekbones trompe l'oeil. But she was there, like a developing photograph, younger than he'd thought, plusher. She might have been the age of his oldest sister, Eloise, who was thirty-two.

"Huh," she said, when she saw him. "You don't belong here."

"I do," he said. Then, "I want to learn how to be a ventriloquist."

She frowned at him. "Good afternoon." Her voice was different on its own, singsongier.

"Good afternoon," he said. "Could you teach me?"

"Really?"

"Yeah," he said.

"Don't tell me how old you are."

"I'm sixteen," he said, knowing he didn't look it. His body hadn't changed yet, but his soul had: this year he had developed delusions of grandeur and a morbid nature and a willingness to die for love; next year, pubic hair and broad shoulders.

"Christ," she said. "Come in."

Her furniture looked serious, antique: she was a grown-up. The sofa was red velvet. He could feel the wood at its heart, as though, if she manipulated it, she could give it a voice and a personality. He thought she was a very good ventriloquist, though he didn't know much about what that entailed. She regarded her puppets with indifference, as though their energy tired her; he'd stared at her mouth, waiting to see her lips move. Eventually they would, a little, gleamingly, like a thin necklace you weren't sure a girl was wearing: you looked for it to appear for the pleasure of having it disappear just afterward.

"I'm not too young," he said.

"If anything you're too old. To be a vent. Most boys pick it up ten or so. Where are your parents?"

"Ithaca."

"Greece?"

"Ithaca, New York," he clarified.

"Yes, I thought you were American."

He decided not to argue with that, though he disagreed. True, he'd been born in the United States, and raised there, but his parents were English, his older sisters were English, every single person he was related to was English. *A dog is a dog though born on a sheep farm,* he told himself.

She said, "Was anybody with you on the boat?"

"No."

She extracted a cigarette from a tin box and lit it with a

large chrome lighter that gave off the scent of fuel. In her act, she struck matches on Willie Shavers's cheek, then smoked while he talked. "You didn't stow away," she said, leaking smoke.

He shook his head.

"But you want to stow away here."

"I can't go back," he said.

"To Ithaca, New York," she said, with an amused expression. "No? Why?"

He had his reasons, but they were ineffable. The fact was he'd planned from the first day to walk off the boat in Southampton, track down one of his sisters—all three of them lived in England: Katie in Sussex, Fiona in Bath, and Eloise in a village in Norfolk called Little Snoring—and ask for sanctuary. But his sisters would no doubt fling him back to his parents. He felt the nap of the velvet sofa, toed the herringbone parquet floor. One of the planks was loose under his sneakered foot, and he knew he could kick it up and out. He wanted to take it with him. All around were pictures of Lottie Stanley with famous people he didn't recognize. He could only tell they were famous, and English: the sideburns, the teeth, the ears. Americans weren't better-looking, they were only more ashamed. He stood to go.

She said, "Sit down, my darling," and appraised him through her winding smoke. On the ship he'd stared at her face for an hour a night, every night for seven. He wasn't used to being looked at, or being called *my darling*. "I've got a home I can't go back to myself. Can you pay weekly rent?"

"A little," he said. He hadn't been paid for his work on the boat—that would have happened on the return—but in his knapsack he had a stack of traveler's checks, his entire savings, withdrawn the day he left.

"Remind me your name?"

"Lenny."

"Oh no," she said. She reached over to an ashtray on a side table to stab out her cigarette, the same gesture she used to punctuate all conversations, including the ones she had on-stage with her several varieties of self. Her hair was a strange tweedy combination of dark and light. "We've already got a Lenny. What's your last name?"

"Valert."

"Jack," she said. "Jack Valert. Suits you."

So he was Jack.

He called his parents six nights later, two in the morning on Lottie's phone, with the knowledge that it would be cheaper at that hour though possibly still astronomically expensive. He'd never made a long-distance phone call in his life. It was the day before he was due to return.

"How are you?" his mother said. "Shattered, I expect."

"I'm in London."

There was a pause. He wondered how much each second would cost. He would have to pay Lottie back.

"Why are you in London?" his mother said at last.

"I'm fine. I'll come back in time for school."

"Better had," said his mother. He could hear his father in the background, and his mother said, her hand over the phone lightly, so he could hear, "It's fine, it's Lenny, it's long-distance."

He'd been Jack for less than a week but Lenny seemed lives ago. Of course his parents wouldn't be alarmed. His youngest older sister had been twelve when they'd moved to New York, already boarding at Downe House in Berkshire. He had a faint memory of her as a womanish child or child-ish woman during school breaks. Fiona and Eloise, too, had gone to boarding school, come to the States for the summers and winter hols, and then graduated and gone on to English lives. Months went by when his parents didn't see the girls. Only Lenny had been raised as an American, sent by his parents to public school—public in the American sense, less impressive, as everything was, in the American sense—as an experiment or a form of surrender. They regarded him as a sort of hanger-on with a pot-metal accent.

"Come when you're able," his mother said to him. "Do let us know your plans."

Lottie gave him her guest room, a narrow space at the back of the flat, with a window at the foot of the bed and a large dresser with a mirror along one wall. "For practice," she said. "That's the only way to learn, practice in the mirror. I can't teach you. I can give you this book, and you can read it, but you'll have to put in the hours."

"Am I really too old?"

"No," she said. "You're young yet. You might make it."

"Were you young?"

"I was, yeah. Ten. My brother had an Archie Andrews figure he'd lost interest in. It's like a language or an instru-ment. Easier when you yourself believe in all the mysteries of the universe. But not impossible afterward. Here." From the top dresser drawer she got out a puppet shaped like a hen, brown with a yellow beak and a drooping red comb.

He put it on his hand. It was tight across the knuckles and abrasive around the wrist.

She turned him by the shoulders so they faced the mirror. Without puppet or pretense, she began to talk without moving her lips. "The hardest letter to say is *B*. Bottle of beer. The boy bought a ball. Barnum brought barnacles by Boston." Then her mouth was mobile again. "The trick is you don't really say it. You say *D*, but you think *B*."

What he had loved about watching her on the boat: the hot cider of her voice against the dry toast of Willie Shavers's, her measured exasperation with him. No: what he loved was big Willie Shavers himself, the glass eyes that looked from side to side, his levering eyebrows, the mystery of his mouth with its stiff lips and painted tongue. Squawkanna the parrot bored him; ditto the yellow tomcat, whose name was Captain Sims. This nameless hen, too. They were mere puppets, animals, sweet, but Willie Shavers unsettled Lenny—Jack, now, he agreed, it suited him—Willie Shavers *upset* Jack in a way that felt very much like love. He realized, in this small room, shirtless, looking at himself in the mirror, that it was Willie he had come for. Willie, who was a bully but yet could be bullied.

Lottie collected his rent and assigned him chores. She was astounded by what he didn't know. "Rinse out the tub after a bath!" she said. Also, "Sit down while you eat." Also, "It's a small flat, nothing can be higgledy-piggledy." Also, "Time to draw the curtains." She believed in putting the physical world in order in a way he would have thought impossible. She was a genius at it. She paid him for lugging her equipment to performances, took the money back for rent and groceries. Her bathroom was long, with a navy-blue toilet and a navy-blue tub with no shower and an entire mirrored wall: maybe she practiced her *B*s and *V*s in every room. He hated standing up from a bath to catch sight of his dripping, naked body, the acne he'd acquired down his breastbone, the allover insufficiency of him. Nights he sat with Lottie on the sofa and they watched TV. English television was shockingly dull. One night they showed a documentary about the '60s. "I slept with her," said Lottie, all of a sudden, when they showed footage of a clothing designer with a short black bob.

"Oh!" said Jack.

"I slept with everyone for a while," she said. Even at home, she favored a kind of dated glitz, rough blue lamé blouses and toreador pants. Her feet were bare, her toenails coral. "Men and women. What about you?"

It occurred to him that he'd shipped himself off to another country so that he could attend to his late puberty alone, like the injured animal he was. Why boys joined the navy in the old days. Why anyone went to sea.

"That's all right," she said. "You don't need to know."

Even later he could not decide whether she was trying to seduce him or be a listening friend.

Think of *B* while saying *D*. Think *B*, say *D*. But all his life he could only say what he thought. He never got any better at it.

He practiced with the hen, whom he loathed. He wouldn't do it in front of Lottie. "The boy bought a ball," he said to his reflection. *The doy dought a doll.* You could try it with *G*s, too. *The goy got a gall.* That at least was a sentence. Maybe he hated the whole enterprise. With the hen on his hand he could feel half his soul, more, leak from his body into the puppet, Siamese twins, the hen the twin with the major organs. The thing he could never do—he saw, looking in the mirror—was hold still. The hen spoke. Jack raised his eyebrows, pecked at the air. He had no talent for making believe. He could not stop being himself.

He could hear his father say it. *You just can't stop being yourself, can you?*

He'd thought he'd feel at home in England. In upstate New York they all were foreigners: despite his accent, Jack's childhood clothes were English, ordered through the mail, and his packed lunches, and his particular snobberies that drove his classmates crazy. He did not have friends at school because he felt superior to everyone, and also inferior.

But London was no better. Maybe he would enlist in the navy, but which one? He didn't want to run away to join the circus: he loathed animals, and contortionists, and the sound of the whip. Perhaps he could sign back on with the crew of the *QE2*, and travel between countries for the rest of his life.

In England he could drink. It was legal. That was stunning. So he did. He accompanied Lottie on gigs: a glamorous one in a fancy house on Holland Park, where Lottie stood in the foyer and people lined the stairs to watch her; a depressing one in a basement theater near Brick Lane where nobody showed up. She always had to sing her song with the parrot, "You're My Bird." She asked Jack to come on television with her, not as a performer but an assistant, who took the figures in and out of their cases. She could have done it herself, she always did, but she dressed him in a suit that made him look like a dummy himself. "Not a dummy," said Lottie, "we don't call them dummies. Ventriloquial figure."

One of these nights he woke up—it was dark—not in the narrow bed in the room with the mirror, but in Lottie's bed, with Lottie. He'd not been so drunk that he couldn't remember what had happened—it would be years before he drank like that—but he could not remember how it had begun, or whether he should be ashamed of himself.

In the morning she was blasé at the breakfast table.

"I hope you feel relieved," she said.

"Yes," he said while thinking, *No.*

"We could get married. Do you need to get married?"

"What do you mean?"

"To stay in England."

"I'm *English*," he said, and she laughed out loud. He had to show her his passport to prove it.

They didn't sleep together every night, just once in a while, and he could never tell whose idea it was, who first inclined a head for a kiss, put a hand to the other's waist. They seemed to be operating each other's bodies. He wondered whether she felt it, too, whether the whole world did. The Sex Act, his father had once called it in an unsuccessful conversation: in which another body compelled your body to move in a lifelike way. It was a negotiation, but you were still yourself, there in your head, more than ever, actually. There were so many things to worry about. You could never lose yourself.

Why had she taken him in? Into her flat; into her bed (beneath which the puppets were stowed, a fact that Jack could never forget). There had to be a reason. An unhappy childhood? A child given up for adoption? She'd been beaten, she'd beaten somebody else, she'd been raised in a religion that forbid idolatry. She had a thing for teenagers. Once, in the middle of the night, he asked her.

"Why do I need a secret to be a terrible person?" she said.

"You're not a terrible person."

No solution to the puzzle of Lottie. No solution to the puzzle of Lenny.

Mornings, he thought about running away from running away, but where could he go? He could call his parents, who would give him the address of one of his older sisters, or some cousins—he remembered visiting an elderly person in a house in Kent when he was seven. But nobody was in London. He went out walking for hours, down Notting Hill Gate to Kensington Gardens, across Kensington Gardens to Exhibition Road, down the old Brompton Road. Everyone in London was from somewhere else. A game he invented: he would look at people, guess where they were from, then get close enough to hear them speak. Shoes and hair were the deadest giveaways. Every so often he would see a woman with a particular expression and he would know without analysis that she was American. The thrill of recognition. He would have to follow her until he heard her talk—to her companion, to a clerk in the chemist's. In the *drugstore*. He was light-footed and invisible, and on this subject he was always right.

He'd been raised by wolves, then delivered to civilization. Then, at the end of the summer, the wolves came back to claim him.

Early September. In Ithaca, New York, his junior year in high school was about to start, but in London Jack was doing his chores, standing at the ironing board in the living room, the only space big enough to unfold it.

"Jack," Lottie called from the door to the flat.

He hadn't seen Fiona for two years, and Eloise for three. The word *relations* lit up in his head: what Eloise and Fiona were to him; what he and Lottie had, in a euphemism his father might have used. *Did you have relations with that revolting woman.* His older sisters had come to rescue him. They were grown-ups and had bank accounts. Five minutes before, he believed his problems were complicated, immense, insoluble; now he understood that every one of them could be dismissed with money. He was so delighted he'd forgotten what the situation looked like: Lottie in an emerald-green satin housecoat, he shirtless and smoking a cigarette over his ironing. Not his own shirt but a tiny blue suit for Willie Shavers. Lottie had promised him to Jack: she didn't like Willie Shavers. You could bend emotion into the cloth puppets; Willie's expressions were purely mechanical. Anyhow, he'd been a gift from her own mentor, a man named Shappy Marks, long dead and—said Lottie—good riddance. But not yet. Jack would have to earn him.

"Lenny," said Fiona, and Eloise said, "Lenny, my God, what happened to you?"

"What do you mean?"

"Look at you," she said. "You're a bag of bones."

"This is Eloise," said Fiona, the kinder one, she was wearing a pink dress with red roses and her hair loose and parted down the middle. "I'm Fiona. Get your things, Len."

Eloise followed him to Lottie's tidy bedroom. Jack was grateful for its orderliness. He wanted Eloise to admire it. From the top drawer of the dresser he extracted a green T-shirt, pulled it on. The bed was made. He felt Eloise study it, the paisley duvet, the two bedside tables, each with its ashtray.

"My God, Len."

"It's all right."

"*All right* is not a phrase I would use, actually," she said. She had the accent all of the family had except him, the voice that Lottie used onstage but not at home: posh, from nowhere. Lottie's actual accent was northern, from Manchester. That was one of the things he had learned in the past weeks. "Not any of this is all right."

"My stuff mostly doesn't fit me, anyhow," he said.

"Leave it, then. Come on. We have to hurry."

Was he just going to walk out with nothing, with nobody? He dropped to the floor and pulled the case marked ws from beneath the bed and zipped it into the duffel he'd arrived with. He'd been promised, but he didn't want to ask; he didn't want to be refused. He swung the duffel behind his back, and it knocked into his legs, it hurt, that's right, everything hurt, he was built of wire and wool.

In the living room, Fiona and Lottie were sitting on the red sofa, each holding a plate with a single untouched jaffa cake. If you didn't know, thought Jack, you would not be able to guess what the two women had in common.

"All right?" Fiona said to them. "Going?" She handed her plate to Lottie. "Good."

"Wait," said Jack. He turned to Lottie. "Do you think," he said, "there's a chance—could I get the extra rent back?"

He was worried she'd get mad. Lottie didn't have much of a temper, but she didn't like being contradicted. She didn't like being asked for favors.

At this, Fiona roared.

"You charged him *rent*?" she said. "You're a grown woman!"

The plates with their cakes, one in each hand, seemed a prank Fiona had played on Lottie to pin her to the sofa. Jack tried to assemble the right emotion for the moment—he might never see her again—and he rummaged through what he had: pity, gratitude, shock, love, disapproval, utter confusion. Her blond hair had been combed into a ponytail. He would never feel the lash of it again.

She said, perplexed, "Well, yes."

Together two-thirds of Leonard Valerts' sisters jostled Leonard Valert himself into a black cab. *Where are we going?*

Airport. *I don't have money.* Daddy's bought you a ticket. *Did he?* Of course. *How did you find me?* Saw you on the telly! *How was I?*

"How *were* you?" said Eloise incredulously. She was sitting on the jump seat, her feet resting on the duffel bag. She stared at him, then said, "You were wonderful."

They were so embarrassed over everything they started to tease him. *Jack*, they said. *Jack, I'm lonely. Where's my monkey?*

"She doesn't have a monkey. She has a cat."

Darling Jack, lovely Jack, come here, I'll stick my hand up you.

Even Jack was laughing. It was horrible and hilarious.

Eloise said in her fancy voice, "What I would like to know is who the fuck is *Jack*."

"Good name for a ventriloquist," offered Jack.

"Better name for a dummy," said Fiona: the nice one.

At Heathrow he opened the stolen case. He'd been so certain he would see Willie Shavers looking up at him he couldn't made sense of it: Captain Sims, the woeful cat; how on earth did he get there? Lottie was meticulous, she said it made a difference, the figures minded where they rested, but it had been careless Jack who'd last packed them up, after a performance in Brighton.

What was the emotion he felt? Less than loss and more than longing. He stared at the slack-jawed cat awhile then shut the case and left it in the airport men's room. Let the bomb squad explode it. Let it linger in lost property forever.

All the way across the ocean he dreamt of Willie Shavers, the little clicking of his mechanisms, his square shoulders, his thick wig. His slumber beneath Lottie's bed. Jack should have known that one of them would have to stay behind.

Thereafter, and for years, whenever he was in public— telling a story at a party, delivering a lecture to undergraduates, holding forth in a meeting—he would feel Willie Shavers, not upon him but in him: sliding glass eyes and deadpan disbelief, quirking eyebrows and carved wooden palate, even the dimple that Willie had and Jack didn't. Even that he could feel upon his cheek. And somewhere behind him, between the small of his back and the nape of his neck (though his body had no other nape and no other small), the ghost hand of Lottie flexed, otherwise uninvolved. She operated no important part of him, nothing at the level of soul or sympathy. Just the bit that allowed him to believe that people might want to hear what he had to say. The part that let him ask strangers for their love, and not care if they said yes.

MISTRESS MICKLE
ALL AT SEA

New Year's Eve in a Rotterdam garret, the whole block blacked out, bottle rockets rattling the casements: Mistress Mickle, villainess of the children's game show *Barnaby Grudge*, off duty and far from home, ate a cold canned hot dog in the dark and pronounced it delicious. These were the last minutes of the old year. She'd come from Surrey to visit her half-brother, Jonas, whom she'd last seen in Boston just before their father had retired to Minorca. Expatriation was the family disease, hereditary: thanks to an immigrant ancestor, they all had Irish passports. The world was their oyster. An oyster was not enough to sustain anyone.

"This happen often?" she asked. "Blackouts, I mean."

"Off-ten?" he mimicked, then he said, "Nah. I don't know what's going on." His Boston accent was thick as ever, but years in England had bent her diction, and she couldn't decide which of them should feel superior. The blackout was in its third hour. She'd hated the darkness at first, but it had gone on so long it had become essential. *Let the New*

Year arrive unelectrified, she thought, *lit only by pyrotechnics.*

Rotterdam did not wait till midnight to celebrate; the enamel tabletop vibrated with the detonations of fireworks, explosion after explosion overhead. It was like life in wartime, if you knew nobody was dying, probably, and the privation would end by morning. She jumped at every salvo; she was a nervous woman. When Jonas fished out a joint she didn't turn him down, though it had been decades. Maybe it would calm her. Last year she would have had a drink, but she didn't drink anymore. She was forty-nine, Jonas forty-two, a shock. He had long, insufficient mousy hair he was trying to drum up into dreadlocks and a thick dark beard he'd trimmed to round perfection. Why couldn't he take care of anything else so well? He was a fuckup. He said so himself. It was as though fucking up were his religion, and he was always looking for a more authentic experience of it: bankrupted by Scientology, busted for selling a stolen antique lamp, fired from an Alaskan cannery for filching salmon, beaten up by a drug dealer—that is, a ham-headed college kid who dealt ecstasy but took only steroids himself. For the past six months, Jonas had lived in this garret, renting the space beneath an Irishwoman's kitchen table, with access to her stove and sink and toilet and, occasionally, herself. The Irishwoman had gone back to Kilkenny, would return tomorrow. Tonight her bed would be occupied by Mistress Mickle. The Irishwoman must never hear of this. Jonas's pallet was still spread out under the table at which they now sat, his pillow at Mistress Mickle's feet.

At eleven thirty the lights came back on.

"Oh good," said Jonas.

"A shame," said Mistress Mickle.

Jonas shrugged. He was a lifelong shrugger. It was the genuflection of the devout fuckup. "Let's go to the street," he said. "Midnight will blow your mind."

Outside they stood by the murky canal that ran down the street like a median strip. All along the block people set off their rockets, nearly dutifully, and gossiped and smoked. She felt the peculiar calm of not understanding the ambient language, a state she loved: it was like having part of your brain induced into a coma.

"Just wait," said Jonas.

What were they waiting for? Oh yes: midnight. Mistress Mickle checked her heart the way she might reach into her handbag for a wallet she was continually certain had been pickpocketed but never was. How was her heart? There, but working? She took her pulse at her neck: steady, fine, though her torso felt percolated. She'd read an article online about women's heart attacks, how they presented differently from men's, how nearly anything (it seemed to Mistress Mickle) might be evidence. Was that pain in her chest, or in her back? In her chest or her breast? What bodily border must a pain cross to enter another bodily meridian? Insomnia could be a symptom, the article said: well, she had that now. She had all the symptoms, though fly-by-night versions. Intimations of symptoms. Not pains, but twinges. Not racing but trotting. She was dying, she was making it up, she wouldn't go to a doctor. She had no natural fear of death, and was vain about this: it was what separated her from the rest of dumb humanity. But she was phobic about embarrassment. That's what the death certificate would cite under cause: *embarrassment, congenital and chronic.*

In the middle of the street, a small boy knelt beside a man with 1970s Elvis sideburns. Not father and son, she didn't think. There was a formality: the man seemed to be the boy's firework godfather, come from far off to teach him how to light a wick. The boy must have been eight. The man must have been a ghost. Together they held a smoldering twist of paper to the fuse and stepped away. Mistress Mickle felt the rocket's rising shrill at the back of her throat, absorbed its pop in her tonsils. It tore itself into three red branches, then faded.

"Fucking *awesome*," Jonas called to the kid.

"Extraordinary," she said, in a four-syllabled, English way. Then, "Yeah, awesome." Already the man and boy were righting the bottle for a new rocket.

"Sixty-five million euro, according to the papers," said Jonas. "That's what the Dutch spent on fireworks this year. Hey, did I tell you? I'm going to apprentice to a hatter."

"You're too old to be an apprentice," she said. Then: "A *hatter*?"

"Felt hats," he said. "They're the next thing. They're coming back."

"Come and went, haven't they?"

He'd been smiling but his smile slipped. Then he smiled more broadly: that his sister might know anything was something he could believe for only seconds at a time. "No," he said. "Real hats. My friend Matthias. He's, like, a genius."

That perfect, round beard: it looked like a hatter's apparatus, come to think of it. A form for the crown of a derby, a tool to bring up the nap of the felt.

"I'll give you more money," Mistress Mickle told him.

"That's not what I'm saying." He had his hands in his greasy mechanic's jacket—he who had never been a mechanic. "I don't need your money."

"Oh?"

"*No*," said Jonas. "That's why I invited you here. To show you. I don't need you anymore. Your help, I mean. Look! I'm standing on two feet." He added, "I think she's pregnant. She *is* pregnant."

"Who? Oh, Irish."

"Siobhan," said Jonas. "Yes."

"So you'll want the money, then."

"Listen to me! That's why hats."

"*Hats*," said Mistress Mickle.

Bickering into the New Year. Typical. They'd heard no countdown, but the turning of the calendar was unmistakable—the syncopation of bottle rockets replaced by whumps, thunderclaps, the crackling aftermath: beauty. Ordinarily Mistress Mickle was afraid of both loud noises and house fires, but the fireworks over Rotterdam—no, she realized, not over *Rotterdam*, the fireworks over this particular neighborhood—she goggled at them. Nobody was sighing in unison, as in the States. There wasn't time to sigh. Every inch of the sky was stitched with flash. Fingers were being blown off, and heart attacks induced, and underneath the explosions you could hear dogs of all sizes bark in agonized registers—but how could Mistress Mickle not marvel? She'd never seen anything like it.

She thought of the invisible woman at the science museum, that mannequin who showed her various systems through her Lucite epidermis: circulatory, nervous, respiratory, reproductive, lit up in turn. The fireworks lit up Mistress Mickle: the blond ones her nerves and the white ones her bones, the red ones her heart, the blue ones her capillaries. They cured her. She was not just fine but better. Soon they'd finish, and she'd be new. But they didn't finish. They kept going. Cured, afflicted, cured, afflicted, cured, until she realized there was no waiting for the end. The Dutch would set them off till the dark was done. Maybe Jonas was right: maybe this was the year he'd stand on two feet. Hope saturated her.

"It's so good to see you," she said to him. She'd learned through the years that saying made it so, at least sometimes. "Really, Jone."

"This is going to be the greatest year of my life," said Jonas, and she said, "Yes, it will, I know it."

Not blond but ginger ale. Not ginger ale but champagne.

Later, in the Irishwoman's bed, she heard a clunk against the roof and realized it was fallout from the night's barrage. Ordinarily she would have stayed awake, waiting for the inevitable smell of disaster. Now she thought, Icarus, Newton's apple, David Bowie, impossible beautiful falling things. A rocket set off hours earlier by the boy in the middle of the street, flown so high it had gone into orbit, circumnavigated the globe, and—like so many flying things—gotten homesick, decided to plummet back.

Should she throw something to the kitchen tabletop, to give her brother the same exhilaration on his bedroll beneath? Would it work?

The table was still scattered with empty hot dog cans. In the Netherlands, they were called *knaks*.

Twelve hours later, Mistress Mickle—her name was Jenny Early, though forty-nine seemed to her too old to be Jenny and too late to be Early—boarded a ferry at the Hook of Holland, headed for Harwich, where her car was parked. She'd lived in England for twenty years, working as an actress, more or less, all that time: in an experimental theater company ("experimental" meant foodstuff and nudity); as a stilt walker in a new-wave circus; as a minor recurring character on *Coronation Street*; as the slowest member of an improv troupe; as a reader to the blind; as a voice-over artist in cartoons and, later, video games; and finally as Mistress Mickle, which involved stilts and a multicolored Victorian dress and yelling, week after week, at an audience of children, from which six players were plucked and protected by a young hero named Micah. (The eponymous Barnaby—actual surname O'Malley—had been fired for sleeping with seventeen-year-olds, which he told the papers was unfair, as there were no seventeen-year-olds in his audience.) Mistress Mickle would attempt to kidnap the children, and even when she

managed to land one in jail—on stilts! In a hoopskirt!—
Micah would always be waiting with the unconvincing card-
board key, which was the size of a leg of lamb. The children
would boo her.

Micah was the beautiful child of a Danish mother and
a Nigerian father, as genial off camera as on, though in real
life guileless, dumb, incapable of outwitting anyone, never
mind a woman so many years his senior. He reminded Mistress Mickle of an alternate Jonas, one whose every slapdash
decision raised him up instead of knocking him down. She
hated Micah for his good luck (though neither Micah nor
Jonas believed in luck: they believed in breezily accepting
the day), and for his consistent love of the children, for his
youth, for the way the game itself was stacked against her.

No children waited for Mistress Mickle on the other side
of her journey, nor husband, nor (at the moment) paramour,
and that was fine. She liked sex and she liked privacy, and
she'd reached her mid-thirties before realizing life could offer her both. The time that living with another person took
up! The small talk! The politeness! Life alone was banal, too,
but at least the banality wasn't narrated.

It was bad for you to say aloud the minor grievances of
the day, the rude bank teller and the gum on the bottom of
your shoe. It was terrible to alter your diet to what another
person liked or didn't: The last man she'd lived with had
hated capers. And so she'd given up capers, until she gave
up the man. His name was Philip. He was a theater direc-
tor who had made fun of her accent, the way she dropped
*t*s in the middle of English expressions and words: *Bee'root.*
Wai'rose. Whi'bait. Qui'right.

All her life she'd felt foreign; landing abroad, she was relieved to assume it as an official diagnosis.

This was a day crossing, but she'd taken an outside cabin, one with a double bed and a single bed and a surprisingly large bathroom with a toilet, shower, sink, and three thick, white towels, more than Jonas had to his name. (What had happened to him, that he lived like that? *Shit happens*, Jonas would say. *Life happens*, Micah would say, *while you're making other plans*.) A free minibar. She ate both chocolates and the bag of potato chips while the boat was still in port. The strange elation of the previous evening was still in her: she felt calmer than she had in ages. The Irishwoman was pregnant. Their family would continue after all! Aunty Mickle! Still stoned, she thought, though she wasn't sure that was true, and she lay down on the single bed, because it was on the right side of the cabin, and the homing device in Mistress Mickle's brain always went right: on busses, on trains, in restaurants. There was a little wall-mounted television; she tuned it to the closed-circuit cameras in the belowdecks kennels. Empty. Empty. Empty. The channel suited her.

Ordinarily she wanted to watch television but couldn't bear to watch. She might see, for instance, an actor in a movie whom she'd met fifteen years ago on a soap: *Now how did he get that break?* She might see young, talentless, gleaming people. It appalled her, the jealousy of her middle age, though it flared up only occasionally, a trick knee. Lumbago, whatever lumbago was. Spiritual arthritis. As a young woman she was (she believed) mostly generous, entirely sane, and the acting jobs she got, the soaps and reenactment shows and cartoon voice-overs, had seemed like good fortune. Now everything was a conspiracy, mean and purposeful, designed to hurt her, and while she knew there were people who saw her in the piebald, pirate-y Mistress Mickle costume on *Barnaby Grudge* and were filled with jealousy themselves, this knowledge didn't comfort her: indeed, when she stopped to contemplate it, she felt demeaned.

Knock it off, she told herself. *New year.* She plumped the pillow. It was a real pillow. It was a good ship. She checked her heart. Beating.

No dogs, still.

She never quite fell asleep, but she observed, as though from a distance, obscure, outlandish thoughts as they alighted: Would Jonas take the Irishwoman's bed, or would he keep obediently to his mat beneath the kitchen table? Why beneath the table? Oh, to avoid being stepped on. A baby in a hat might crawl by, too—now, what did that mean? she asked herself in an Irish accent. The sea grew rough: every now and then a wave lifted the boat up and set it down with a minor clunk, and the back room of her brain thought, *Ah, the plane has landed.*

She sat up after thinking this for the third time. Not plane, boat. The television showed its series of empty kennels. It looked like a prison break: *I don't know, Sarge, the cells were all full half an hour ago.*

Between the beds a large, lozenge-shaped window. A porthole. A window that would allow nobody to spy on you. She regarded the polished green sea cut through with unpolished white foam. She heard an ululating child run down the corridor outside: toddler Doppler effect. Other than that, the cabin was the most complete privacy one could imagine while still surrounded by hundreds of people, and superb. There was nothing she didn't like. How to fully enjoy it? She had an urge to transgress, to drink the pygmy minibar red wine, then the white, then the two cans of Heineken, to strip and press her nakedness against the porthole.

Who would know? Some unseen sailor with a telescope. Satellites. Aliens. Nobody. Fish.

She didn't drink anymore. Hours to go before Harwich. She needed to get out.

The public areas were on deck nine. She'd been on shitty ferries, but this was a nice one. Coffee bars, wine bars, a cafeteria, even a fancy restaurant with a three-course prix fixe menu. Most of the passengers (there weren't many) seemed to be Middle Eastern Muslims, the women in chadors and head scarves, a pair of tiny girls hidden in floor-length dresses, the men in blue jeans. *Of course*, thought Mistress Mickle: everyone else was too hungover on New Year's Day to chance a ferry. You had to be from a nondrinking people to survive. Or naval: she had navy on both sides of the family; she never got sick. Still, the roughness of the sea was a low-level prank beneath her feet: three steps fine, and then the deck rose up quick. At the far end of the cafeteria a white-haired man pulled a clattering child's toy, a dragon that smacked its jaws as it rolled along. The man wore a round embroidered Chinese hat and pants that showed his ankles, and he tweaked balloons into dogs and handed them to children. She supposed she and he were members of the same tribe, or the same theoretical union. *Keep your distance*, she thought at him.

Where was Jonas now? He'd ridden the bus with her to the central train station, used her credit card to buy her ticket to the port. He was going to be a father. (She resolved to believe it.) Fathers should not sleep beneath kitchen tables. He needed money. She would send it happily, without negotiation or expectation.

She walked through a door out onto an open deck at the end of the boat. Not end. Stern. She walked to the stern of the boat past the smokers and stared sternly out. The sharp salt air did her some good, though the smokers all looked fucked off with the cold. Why she'd quit: after the ban in restaurants and pubs, smoking had become a standing endeavor, and she had no interest in smoking upright. She stood at the rail and looked at the water.

She thought—as she often did when she saw an opportunity—of doing away with herself. Wait till the deck cleared so nobody would witness her. Jump in. Drown. How long would it take till she was noticed missing? She might be an enduring mystery, like Judge Crater (US) or Lord Lucan (UK). You waited to disappear till nobody watched you go. Otherwise you'd be only a dull suicide.

This was a lifelong habit. It didn't feel suicidal but the opposite, a satisfying of a not-quite-urge. Whenever she moved to a new place, for instance, she looked for the support she'd hang herself from. In her current house, a barn conversion, there were beams everywhere, though the best was in the kitchen, with an iron hook. Finding the spot calmed her. She didn't want to kill herself, but she did want to think about it. After all, she wasn't afraid of death.

She decided to live forever or as long as possible. She would learn to be a better person, for her niece's sake. (Why niece? She couldn't imagine Jonas as the father of a son, was all.) Today it felt entirely possible. Was this optimism? Was this what Micah and Jonas felt?

The water behind a boat is the deepest wishing well in the world: It has drag and intention. Throw your dreams into it. If they don't pull you in and drown you, perhaps they'll come true.

On a table inside she found a flyer. CHILDREN'S ENTERTAI-MENT, it said, 2:30 IN THE KID ZONE! MAGIC, BALLOONS! *Well*, she thought. *Why not.* The boat appeared so empty she imagined nobody else might show up, the sea sufficiently turbulent that any children were lying flat and sipping warm water. Professional courtesy, one children's performer to another. She would be his audience.

But the KID ZONE!, a glassed-in space just beyond the cafeteria, was full. With palpable delight, a young white woman (English, Mistress Mickle was pretty sure) watched her two-year-old daughter waddle up to the man in the Chinese hat: how lucky, the mother clearly thought, that the world had the chance to experience her child! A plump red-headed boy clutched a model of the very boat they were on, purchased from the gift shop. Two-thirds of the audience seemed to be one large Muslim family, or several families traveling together: kids in the front row, a couple of men leaning against the far wall, four young women in matching robin's-egg-blue head scarves who could have been mothers to the audience, or older sisters. Not all the teenage girls wore head coverings, so probably they weren't all related. They were different strains. *Denominations.* The God of one allowed you to show your neck, and the God of another allowed you to wear slacks.

Where were they from? Somewhere in the Middle East. Even if she heard them speak, she wouldn't know. She had a bum ear: probably why the height of her acting career was a villain on a children's game show. Dutch sounded like German to her, and Portuguese like Russian. Were they Iraqi, Yemeni? Then one of the teenage boys sighed and said to a teenage girl, in a voice of dread and Birmingham, "This is taking for*ever*. I wish we'd flown."

"Fly, then," said his sister. "Go ahead."

Returning home. At sea with the English, as per usual.

One elderly woman, tucked in a porthole frame, clapped impatiently at a small boy who'd stood up and started to wander. (She was from elsewhere, surely, the original cutting on the family tree.) (They were at sea, they were all from elsewhere.) The boy was little, in elasticized jeans with prominent belt loops. Mistress Mickle wanted to set him in her own lap, whisper in his ear, *Shh, let's watch the show*, lay her cheek against his hot head. She did feel inclined toward some children, little ones, those not yet taught by television to hate her. The boy's older sister, a girl of six, knit her already comically serious eyebrows and grabbed him by the waist and gave him a good slug on the arm. Then, as though overcome with love, she seized and kissed him.

Mistress Mickle sat on the floor by the door.

The man in the Chinese hat turned to the audience. He held up to the light three balls filled with glittery fluid. Wordlessly he began juggling. Three balls was relatively easy, Mistress Mickle knew from her years with Circus a Go-Go, and then thought: *but hard on a pitching boat*. With a military *hup*, he popped the third ball, then again, again, till all the children were watching.

"Hello," he said. "I am the Magnificent Jimmy." He had a London accent, despite the Chinese hat and Moroccan slippers. Then he said, more firmly, "Hello!"

"Hello," the audience answered, the way you might greet a friendly lunatic in the park.

"That's rubbish, that is," said the Magnificent Jimmy. *"Hello!"*

"Hello!" the children said, loudly this time. He gave a satisfied nod.

At juggling he was fine, he was acceptable, he was *delightful*: she had forgotten what a good audience member she was. How she liked *looking* at people who wanted only to entertain, no matter how talented—or untalented—they might be. That was why she'd begun acting in the first place, to be regarded by strangers in the way she did them, with a kind of open narrative love that made up stories. Had he done this all his life? Did he live on board? No: he lived in a bedsit in Harwich. He'd hoped to be a famous magician but had never thrown that first leg over the gate of success. His elderly mother was still alive. He took care of her.

The toddler girl threatened the Magnificent Jimmy's knees as her mother looked on in admiration; the redheaded boy kept trying to go back of him, as though the Magnificent Jimmy himself were a trick to get to the bottom of.

"Here we go," said the Magnificent Jimmy, "keep your eye on the blue ball," and then the blue ball got away from him. It rolled toward the antsy little boy, who caught it.

"Thank you, mate," said the Magnificent Jimmy, "toss 'er here," and the boy did. "You're a very naughty blue ball," the Magnificent Jimmy told the blue ball. "Don't ever leave me again."

His balloon-animal skills were terrific, balloons inside balloons, all blown up by his own lungs, no tacky hand pump. "I'll do this in one go," he said, and he filled a green balloon with one long breath. "I like to do it to annoy the smokers. Not bad for sixty-seven, eh?" An alien in a helmet. A dachshund who'd swallowed a meatball. A red Jelly Baby. "All my dogs are green poodles," he said. "Reason being: when I was eleven, I painted the neighbor lady's poodle green, and my father laughed. First good response I ever got from the man. Therefore, green poodles."

She hoped he'd make balloons for everyone; she felt nervous for the children who didn't have one yet. When you were a child you believed yourself special, deserving, and every piece of evidence to the contrary broke your heart. As an adult, the same was true. She hated when magicians asked for child volunteers, as the Magnificent Jimmy did: she felt swamped by the longing that rose up. Little kids put up their hands, eighteen-month-olds: they didn't know they didn't have a chance.

And yet Mistress Mickle loved the Magnificent Jimmy. It was a condescending love, she knew; she was Mistress Mickle, on television: you could buy a doll of her; he was the Magnificent Jimmy, sixty-seven and performing on a ferry. Perhaps she could get him an appearance on *Barnaby Grudge*. Or some other CBeebies program: she would talk to them. She would change his luck. He had the melancholy edge of a man acquainted with the dark thoughts of the back of the boat, someone whose life had not quite panned out. Maybe she would invite him to the excellent privacy of her cabin. Her heart scuttled, a sign she was actually considering it. Today she might do anything.

"All right," said the Magnificent Jimmy, "this doesn't work for everyone, but it does for some." He pulled out a large, black-and-white disc on a stick, set it spinning. "Stare at the center. The very center. Keep staring."

Was he hypnotizing them? She hoped so. She wanted to be changed. She would stand and do anything the Magnificent Jimmy commanded. For once she would be *susceptible*. So she concentrated, the good student, on the gyre of the disc. It seemed to go on for hours.

"Stare. Stare. Stare—now look at me!"

Gasps. Laughter. A teenage girl said, "Oh! Look at his head!"

For Mistress Mickle, nothing.

"Now, some people might have seen my head getting bigger," said the Magnificent Jimmy, and she was stabbed with jealousy: she wanted to snatch that vision straight out of the heads of the underserving children. "Did you see it?" he asked the girl with the serious eyebrows. The girl nodded, looked thoughtful, and opened her mouth—to vomit, it turned out.

She was only the first. The sea had grown furious, but nobody had quite noticed. You could tell the mothers from the sisters then: the sisters giggled and flinched, the mothers leapt forward, hands open—for what?

"Oh, sweethearts," said the Magnificent Jimmy. "Poor

things. There's your mother, darling. All right, all right, she'll take care of you."

But what about me? thought Mistress Mickle. She felt a dull and radiating pain in her jaw, and she stood, and threw up, and fled.

She should have gone back to the cabin—to the shower, the clean towels, her full suitcase—but she had the idea that she shouldn't be sealed in a box. She should be near other people, just in case. So she pulled her coat over her dress (not an unremitting mess: she had vomited directly into a pool of vomit) and stumbled to the open air. The cold was good, and she felt a flare of the day's joy. Then it passed and she felt doom.

Throw yourself in. Who would care?

Over the years, she'd gone through the list: her parents (they'd get over it), Jonas (him, too), various lovers (who would mourn her or not, but their lives would not be ruined), her soap opera character (if she were currently playing a character, and if such character were consequential enough for her absence to matter, she would be gently written out of the show).

Wait. Wait, now.

There was no writing Mistress Mickle out of *Barnaby Grudge*. Was it the water or the realization that made her anxious? The wind boxed her ears. She drew her shoulders up to shield them. She was short of breath.

How would they explain it to the children? Would they simply hire another tall woman with a deep voice and an

aptitude for stilts? Would they offer young actresses her cor-
set like Cinderella's slipper?

The parents of those children: they would be the ones
who'd hate her.

They replaced Barnaby. They will replace you.

"Ahoy!" came a voice from behind. She turned. The Magnificent Jimmy, in a pillowy orange Michelin Man down coat,
his ankles bare to the wind and his little velvet slippers hor-
rid, splattered. "You all right?"

She nodded, though it was a lie. "Quite a finish," she
said. "Was that arranged?"

He laughed. "Never had a show end like that before! A
chundering ovation. Where's your child?"

A reasonable question. She looked around before she remembered. "I don't have one."

"Oh," he said, puzzled. Then, "Me neither."

She'd always thought it was good for a children's performer to be childless. Otherwise you'd meet children thinking, *Not as smart as mine.* Or worse: *smarter than mine,
lovelier than mine.* She judged every piece of art sent to the
show: *Martin, age six, of Sussex, you drew that with your foot.
Penny, age nine, of Walthamstow, that's the worst fucking fairy
I ever saw: it looks like a wingéd footstool.*

"I hate children," said Mistress Mickle, with the force of a
criminal confession. It echoed the same way. "Never wanted
them."

The Magnificent Jimmy appeared stricken, and cold. "Oh.
Pity. I did. We did. Wanted them. But it didn't happen for
me and the wife."

Mistress Mickle felt dizzy. Her whole back ached. Panic.

She should say something. Ask for help. Then, "You were great. You were really great."

"Thanks very much," he said, but he was turning away, going back in. "You all right, then?"

"Listen," she said, "I can get you work."

"I've got work."

"No, I mean—I'm—"

"I know who you are," he said, and went back in.

She sat in a chair and pulled her coat around her and threw up again, and then, without knowing it was going to happen, without a single premonition, she shit her pants: it was the most awful and bewildering feeling—all that warmth against her cold, sodden skin. Mistress Mickle was dying. Jenny Early was dying. Not of embarrassment after all. She was embarrassed, but that wasn't what was killing her.

She was afraid.

Of death? Yes, she felt the edge of it, like a metal box buried in the dirt of the yard that's worked its way up. All these years she hadn't been brave about death but incredulous. On the most fundamental level, and despite all the evidence to the contrary, she hadn't believed in it. She might have believed when her parents died—her father of a heart attack, her mother of liver cancer—because she did grieve them, miss them. Eventually she cheered up, and it didn't feel as though it were time healing all wounds, but an incorrect assumption made correct. They weren't dead, they were elsewhere. Of course, she'd had her mother cremated; she'd gone to the funeral arranged by her father's second wife. Then she'd seen neither parent for years. But there was no part of her that believed in their permanent absence. That's why heaven. Heaven was invented not because people believed but because they didn't.

She could feel the boat of people behind her. They were in the wine bar or the cinema. They were wiping the brows and mouths of their children. She, she was facing all they'd sailed away from. Jonas in the garret, the Irishwoman home and coming up the stairs, everywhere the tatters of fireworks. Her money would go to Jonas. Her nice house. It would save him or ruin him. The ferry was an hour from Harwich, but she'd never see Harwich again. The crew would find her body an hour after docking.

She tried to say something to the air. She felt like one of those Rotterdam dogs, barking and barking while the humans laughed and set off explosions. *Don't you understand, I'm not unhappy, I'm warning you, I'm telling you this is wrong, dangerous, calamitous: the sky will fall around your ears at any moment. Stop looking up and laughing. It isn't cute. It isn't beautiful. It's the end of the world.*

And then—how do we know this? reader, we have it on the highest authority—the ocean came calm and smooth, and Mistress Mickle's heart did likewise, and she felt entirely better, and safe.

BIRDSONG FROM
THE RADIO

"Long ago," Leonora told her children, and the telling was long ago, too, "I was just ordinary." Of course they didn't believe her. She was taller than other mothers, with a mouthful of nibbling, nuzzling teeth, and an affectionate chin she used as a lever. Her hair was roan, her eyes taurine. Later the children would look at the handful of photographs of their mother from the time, all blurred and ill lit, as though even the camera were uncertain who she was, and they would try to remember the gobbling slide of her bite along their necks, her mouth loose and toothy on a shoulder. The threat of more. She was voracious. They could not stop laughing. *No! No! Again!*

Children long to be eaten. Everyone knows that.

"Don't you want to devour that child?" Leonora asked. "Oh, look at that bottom. I am, I'm going to bite it. I'm going to eat that child whole."

(To speak of love as cannibalism! She would have thought

it bizarre herself, before her marriage, but here were the children, Rosa, Marco, Dolly, plump loaves of bread, delicious.)

Those were the days just before busses replaced the trolley lines. The children could hear from their bedroom windows the screech of the streetcars up the hill. Their father ran his family's radio manufacturers, and there were radios in every room of the house, pocket and tabletop, historic cathedrals. His name was Alan. "Poor Alan," Leonora called him, and they both understood why: he was in thrall to his wife. He was a very bus of a man, practical and mobile, and he left the children to Leonora, who had a talent for love, as he had a talent for business.

Winters she took the children tobogganing. Summers they piloted paddleboats across the city pond. She never dressed for the weather. No gloves, no sun hats, no shorts, no scarves. She was always blowing on her fingers or fanning her shirt against her torso. Sunburn, windburn, soaking wet with rain. The children, too. Other mothers sent them home with hand-me-down mittens and umbrellas.

Not surprising, said those mothers later: she never took care of her children.

Rosa, Marco, Dolly: Leonora took them to see the trolleys the last day they ran. She wore a green suede coat, the same color as the trolleys, in solidarity. The coat closed with black loops, which Leonora assured her children were called *frogs*.

"It's raining," said Leonora. "The frogs will be happy."

"Those aren't frogs," said Marco. He was five, the age of taxonomy.

"They are," said Leonora. "I promise. And my shoes are alligator."

"Why are we watching the streetcars?" asked Marco.

"There's no beauty in busses," Leonora said. "A bus can go anywhere it likes. A trolley is beautiful."

"Oh yes," said Rosa, who was seven, "I can see."

Leonora was as doleful as if the streetcars had been hunted into extinction. They were lovely captives who could not get away, and they left only their tracks behind.

Her coat fastened with frogs; her shoes were alligator. Perhaps she was already turning into an animal.

The children grew bigger, and bony. Leonora grew worse about love: she demanded it. She kissed too hard. She grabbed the children by the arms to pull them close. "You *seized* me," said Dolly, age six. "Why did you seize me so?"

"I was looking for a place to nibble," said Leonora. Dolly was a skinny girl.

Leonora bit. She really did now. Moments later, contrite, writhing, she would say, "The problem is I love you so. I do. Can I be near you? Do you mind?"

Later, when the neighbors discussed what had happened, exactly, to Leonora, they couldn't decide. The story of her family was long and sad—a great-grandfather had lived three decades in an asylum; an aunt had killed herself—and the story had not reached its conclusion: here was Leonora's chapter. She missed her children, who were growing up. She had been, from a distance, a bonny mother, thin, patient, and now she thickened, and coarsened, and you could hear her shriek from all the windows of the house. She had gone mad, or was going.

The doctors prescribed her pills, which she refused to take.

She still tried to eat her children, but they were afraid of her. So she had to sneak. The weight of her as she sat on the edge of their beds in the middle of the night was raptorial: ominous yet indistinct. At any moment, the children thought, she might spread her arms and pull them from the sheets through the ceiling and into the sky, the better to harm them elsewhere. The children took to sleeping in the same bed. Rosa, Marco, Dolly. Too old to sleep together, but they had to. They chose a different bed every night, and lay quietly, as they heard her go from pillow to pillow, the unfurling flump of the sheets like the wings they thought they could see on her back.

"Come back to bed," said Poor Alan from the hallway in a terrified voice. "Come listen to the radio and fall asleep." The top of his head was bald. The children could see the bathroom light pool in a little dent in his scalp, just below his summit.

The children had radios in their rooms. He snapped one on, to the classical station, to calm them down. "You never need be lonely with a radio!" he always said, but they knew that wasn't so. A radio station was another way grown-ups could talk to you without ever having to listen.

It was Rosa who told Poor Alan that they had to go. She was fifteen. "We're leaving," she told him. "You can come if you want to. But Marco and Dolly and I are going." Then, seeing his face, "We'd like you to come."

"She needs help," he said.

"She won't get it."

He nodded. "How will we manage?"

"We're not managing now," said Rosa. "In a year I'll get my license. I'll drive the little kids to school." The little kids! She was only two years older than Marco, who was three years older than Dolly.

"What will happen to your mother?" said Poor Alan, wringing his hands.

"Whatever it is, it's already happening," said Rosa. "I can't watch anymore."

"She's a wonderful mother. You must remember that."

"I don't," said Rosa.

He wasn't a bad man. He could be mistaken for thinking it was a war, an ancient one, and that she would fight against the rest of them as long as she was near. In the autumn he took Rosa and Marco and Dolly to a new house, and Leonora was left behind. He arranged for her disability checks. He did not take her off the bank account.

"If you get help, we'll come back," he told her.

Poor Alan hired a nanny, Madeline, a jug-eared, freck-led beauty. A good girl, as her father later described her to news cameras. She picked the children up at the end of every school day and brought them to the house. Rosa worshipped her; Dolly and Marco merely loved her. This went on for five months until the day after Madeline's twenty-first birthday, when she woke up in the middle of the day still drunk from the first legal cocktails of her life, start of February, drove to the school, got the children into the car, and found the car was too hot, and as she tried to wrench her wool coat off one shoulder, and as she felt the last of the black Russians muscle through her veins, and as she hit a patch of black ice, she understood there would be an accident. She could see the children hurt in the back seat. The windshield gone lacey. Herself, opening the door, and running away, away, away. *When the car stops, I'm going to leg it*, and that was the last thought Madeline or any of them ever had.

No children, thought Leonora. She had intended to get herself upright and go looking for them. She should have eaten them when she could.

For a while she tried to distract herself with the radios. Each wore Poor Alan's family name like a crest on the pellicle of the speaker. She went from room to room and turned them on, but then she thought she could hear—behind the sonorous daylong monologue of the news station, or the awful brightness of Vivaldi on the classical station, or jokes cracked by a disc jockey named after an ancient king—the voices of her children. She tried to tune them in. You had to use the volume and the tuning knob in mincing little oscillations. Then, there it was: the tootling rhythm of Dolly's conversation. Rosa humming at the back of her throat as though ready to defiantly swallow the sound should someone walk into the room. Marco sighing before he explained something. She wondered whether they each had a station, Dolly, Marco, Rosa. Maybe they had different radios, even. No: they would be cuddled up together in one frequency, the way they liked.

But she could never tune them in clearly, and slowly the noise behind the newscast turned feral, howling, chirping, shrieking: a forest empty of children. Then she knew they were gone. The radios wouldn't twist off tight enough. The voices of strangers leaked through, no matter how hard she turned the knob. She unplugged the radios, knocked the batteries from the backs. She could still hear that burble, someone muttering or the sound of an engine a block away.

She lay in bed. At her ear hummed the old clock radio, with the numbered decagons that showed their corners as they turned to indicate that a minute had ended, or an hour, the hum a little louder then. She felt her torso, where her children would have been, had she managed to eat them.

Not everyone who stops being human turns animal, but Leonora did.

It was time to leave the house. The top of her back grew humped with ursine fat, and she shambled like that, too, bearlike through the aisles of the grocery store at the end of the street. She shouldered the upright fridges full of beer; she sniffed the air of the checkout lanes. Panda-eyed and eagle-toed and lion-tailed, with a long braid down her back that snapped as though with muscles and vertebrae. Her insides, too. Animals of the dark and deep. Her kidneys dozing moles; her lungs, folded bats. The organs that had authored her children: jellyfish, jellyfish, eel, eel, manatee.

I am dead. I am operated by animals.

Her wandering took her to the bakery, where every Saturday morning of their early childhood, she'd taken her children, to let Poor Alan sleep in. In the angled case she saw the loaves of challah. She saw something familiar in the shape.

"Can I help you?" said the teenager behind the counter. His T-shirt had a picture of the galaxy on it, captioned YOU ARE HERE.

She tapped the glass in front of the challah. "Please," she said, and he pulled a loaf out, and she said, "I don't need a bag."

He had already started angling the loaf into the bag's brown mouth. Who didn't need a bag for bread?

"I don't need a bag," she repeated. She counted out the money and set it down. "Just the paper."

He handed it self-consciously across the counter. When it was in her hands she adjusted the paper around it, admired the sheen of the egg wash, its placid countenance. Then she carried it to a table in the window and spread out the wax paper and set the loaf upon it.

Marco. She saw his sleeping baby self in the shape of the bread. Knees and arms akimbo, head turned, as always, to the left. The girls had cast different shadows. She put her hand on the loaf to check for oven warmth. Not on the surface. Maybe at the heart. Later she wouldn't care what people thought of her, she'd cradle the loaf in her arms before eating, but now she patted the bread, and then, with careful fingers, pulled it apart. That sense of invading a privacy that is then offered up to you. Yeast, warmth, sweetness: a child. Her mouth was full with it, and then her head, and throat, and stomach. She felt the feral parts of her grow sleepy and peaceable.

Thereafter, every morning she went to the bakery and bought a challah and pretended it was one of her children. She knew she could never say this aloud. Rosa slept with her bottom in the air. Dolly, alone of the children, needed to be swaddled. Marco, akimbo. She carried the day's loaf in her arms to the table. She patted it. Then she ate it. Not like an animal. Knob by knob, slowly: one loaf could last her four hours, washed down with water from the waxy paper cups the bakery gave away for free.

That was her nourishment. She lived on bread and good manners and felt sick with her children.

The new mothers of the neighborhood wished the bakery would throw the bulky unkempt woman out. As they wished they felt guilty, because they were trying to teach their children tolerance. But then they looked at the angled case. The center bay was filled with glittering sugared shortbread cookies, decorated according to the season. Hearts, shamrocks, eggs, flags, leaves, pumpkins, turkeys, candy canes, hearts again. Evidence: bakeries were for children, and children were frightened of Leonora. (A trick of the radio again. The children were only tuned to their mothers' fear.)

Sometimes a mother and child would walk by her table, and Leonora could see the rictus of judgment on the mother's face.

"Say hello, Pearl," the mother would tell her child, and Pearl, dutifully, would say hello, and Leonora would wave. She knew that the mother was thinking, *Thank God she doesn't know what I'm thinking.*

Those children neither pained nor interested her. They weren't her lost ones. But every now and then a Pearl or a Sammy would smile at her, and even giggle, and she would, she would want a nibble, a kiss, in the old way. A raspberry blown on a neck, a kiss with a bite at its heart: *nibble, nibble, yum.* They weren't hers, but they were sweet. But if you were the mother of dead children, that was over. You weren't allowed.

On those days she ordered a second loaf of bread, which she dragged home and tore apart.

Five years passed like nothing. She was recognized in the neighborhood as the monument she was, constructed to memorialize a tragedy but with the plaque long since dropped off. She was Leonora. Her name had survived, because the bakery workers remembered it, but that was all. Nobody imagined that she was a mother. She was (anyone who saw her presumed) a person who had always been exactly thus, poisoned, padded, eyes sunk into her face. She existed only at the table, eating bread in her finicking way. She spoke to the people behind the counter. That was all. Some of them were patient, and some of them weren't.

Then one day a man came into the bakery, caught her eye, and smiled.

Poor Alan, she thought reflexively, but then she remembered Poor Alan was dead, though he'd remembered her in his will and set up a trust to take care of her. This man wore a green wool hat like a bucket. The hat looked expensive, imported. He pulled it from his head and revealed a mop of white hair. No, he never was Poor Alan, who'd lost his hair long before it faded. But she did know the man. He sat down across from her. The tabletop was Formica, the green of trolleys.

"Mike Wooster," he said.

"Hello, Mike Wooster," said Leonora. She could smell her own vile breath. She slept in a bed and washed herself, but she did not always remember to brush her teeth. Why would she? She scarcely used them.

He bounced the hat around on his fists. Then he set it in front of him. She had a sense he wanted to drop it over the remains of the day's bread: Dolly this time. He said, "I'm Madeline's father."

She heard the present tense of the sentence.

Everything about him was rich and lulled. "I heard you came here," he said. "That bread good?"

She tore off a brown curve. A cheek, a clenched hand. She sniffed at it before she pushed it in her mouth.

He cleared his throat. "We're having a memorial service. And my wife and I and our kids—well, we thought of you." He picked the hat back up, brushed some flakes of challah from the brim. "I've thought of you." He said that to the hat, then got hold of himself. "Every single day I've thought of you. You know," he said, "they turned my daughter into a monster, too."

The alcohol, the coat, the ice. Everyone said that if one of those things hadn't been true, they never would have crashed. "Too?" she said.

The animals of her body were roaring back to life. They—whoever *they* were—had not turned Leonora into a monster. They had erased her. Newspapers, television, the terrible gabbling radio, which spoke only of the children's father, the left-behind man, the single parent. That poor man, looking after his children. To lose all of them at once.

Poor Alan had held a funeral, had invited her. Though

he'd asked her to come to the front, she'd sat alone at the back of the church—a *church!* Since *when!*—drunk and unmoored. Nobody spoke to her. She was a mother who'd let her children go, a creature so awful nobody believed in her. She'd had to turn herself into a monster in order to be seen.

"Madeline never got a chance," said Mike Wooster. "To redeem herself. But you could. You could be redeemed."

She laughed, or part of her did, a living thing sheltered in a cave inside of her. "Redeemed," she said. "Like a Skee-Ball ticket."

"Like a soul. Your *soul* can be redeemed."

"Too late," she said. "Soul's gone."

"Where?" he said.

"Where do you *think*?" she said.

At that he took her hand. "This only feels like hell," he said. "I know. I do know."

She shook her head to refuse his sympathy: she could smell the distant desiccation of it. *No.* Why had he come here? She could not be redeemed, a coupon, a ticket. He had a dead child, too. She could feel it twitching through his fingers, the sorrow, the guilt, like schools of tiny flicking fish who swim through bone instead of ocean. He was not entirely human anymore, either. Indeed, she could hear the barking dog of his heart, wanting an answer. Her heart snarled back, but tentatively.

If she accepted his sympathy, then she would have to feel sorry for him. She would have to *transcend*. Some people could. They could forgive and rise above their agony.

She could feel the turning of her organs in their burrows, and she felt an old emotion, one from before. Gratitude.

She was thankful to remember that she was a monster. Many monsters. Not a chimera but a vivarium. Her heart snarled, and snarled, and snarled. She tried to listen to it.

"The thing," Leonora told Mike Wooster, and she pulled her hand from his, "is that you can't unbraid a challah."

"No?" he said. "Well, I'd guess not."

"Would you like some?" she asked.

He looked at the rubble of the day's loaf. "Oh no. No, that's yours."

"Let me get you one. Please."

"I don't need—"

Leonora said, rising, "It will be a pleasure to watch you eat."

THE GET-GO

Sadie's mother was tall and narrow, with a long braid down her back, black when Sadie was very little, then silvery, then silver, an instrument to measure time, an atomic clock. Her father had been tall, too, both he and the mother the tallest members of short families. In photographs and at reunions, they loomed. Everyone was happy when they had a short child: they'd decided to fit in after all. Sadie was small and plump and blond, and when she was nine, her father died, and it was just the mismatched mother and daughter, a different kind of sight gag.

Years later Sadie brought Jack home to meet her mother, Linda Brody, who still lived in the green house on a hill in Swampscott, with its view of the ocean and its cyclone fence. Windy on that hill. All his life Jack had felt like an interloper. He might as well, he decided, interlope on purpose. The doorbell was a little button with an orange light so you could see it in the dark. It was daylight. Sadie pushed it.

"You can't go in?" Jack asked.

"It's her house," said Sadie. She opened the storm door and her mother opened the front door, a minuet, and mother and daughter met on the threshold. They hugged each other so long Jack wondered whether he should leave. Finally, they disentangled, Linda in her apple-red cowl-neck sweater, Sadie in her cherry-red winter coat. Linda offered Jack her hand and said, "Linda," still gazing, lovestruck, at Sadie.

She's basically a hermit, Sadie had told him, and Jack had imagined a lady lighthouse keeper, a kind of nun—not a *nun* nun, since Linda was Jewish, but a woman of the book, devoted to reading. She was a high school librarian; she'd gone back to school for it once widowed. Here she was, with her cheekbones and her hair in its braid, her little house bound up in aluminum cladding the pale green of an after-dinner mint.

"Come in," she said, "before the wind takes you."

She strong-armed the storm door open so that Jack and Sadie could step inside, but she seemed unable to look at him. In his life he'd been ignored, but in ways that had made him feel invisible. The way Linda Brody turned from him, he felt blindingly bright, gargantuan. He took himself to the window and watched Sadie's mother unzip Sadie's down coat, take it off shoulder by shoulder, elbow by elbow, wrist by tender wrist. Down the hall was Sadie's childhood bedroom, and Jack understood that he wouldn't see it this visit, might never: it would be shut to him forever.

"Let me look at you," Sadie's mother said to Sadie, and set her hands on Sadie's hips, and frowned.

"Okay, Mom."

"It's a lovely house," Jack offered interlopingly, though it wasn't. There was a general disorder to the room, books on every table, venetian blinds at odd angles to window frames. The furniture looked as though it had been bought all at once from a catalog. There was not a piece of art on the walls. Jack gestured at the window. "Look at that view!" Truthfully the view was only good in that you could see a pennant of ocean in the right upper corner. The rest was taken up with hedges, the across-the-street house, television aerials, telephone wires.

"It's nice," Linda agreed. "You need a new coat, Sadie. Let's go shopping: you can pick one out."

"I'll buy you a coat," said Jack.

"We'll go to Lord & Taylor's," said Linda.

Her father's death had bound her to her mother. How could Jack not have known this? Everything that Sadie had told Jack about Linda, her height, her seriousness, her occasional unkindness, the way she fussed over Sadie's weight, couldn't carry a tune but sang, couldn't remember the name of any of Sadie's friends—none of them had prepared him for this truth. Sadie's mother loved her unnervingly. Not in a way that meant she'd love him, too. The opposite. Their love was a piece of furniture designed for two people only. Their love was an institution that barred men. Their love was *love*, provable and testable, solid, documented in any number of ways. What Jack and Sadie had was something different, built quickly, a lean-to, like all young love.

He'd imagined he'd walk into Linda's life through Sadie's door. That was how it had worked in his family: Sadie belonged to him; she arrived with him as luggage, to be understood only as a part of his life. He saw that this wouldn't work with Linda. He would have to come around the other side and talk his way in.

He left the window and sat in a leatherette armchair seemingly made of the skins of Gideon bibles. It sighed under his weight. "Oh!" he said. "Jordan almonds!" He reached over and took a handful from the bowl on the glass coffee table, and Linda lunged and slapped his forearm, really *slapped* it, and said, in the voice of a shocked dog owner, "*No.*"

Then she put her hands to her temples, contrite. "I just always get those for Sadie," she said miserably. "She loves them. They're harder to find than they used to be."

It had hurt. She'd meant it. He looked at Linda, then at Sadie, and understood that they were all going to pretend this hadn't happened. He had the almonds in his fist, which he unfurled. The pastel coating had started to transfer to his palm. "Of course," he said. "You have them."

That was the start of their lives together. It went on for years. A mistake, to go to the house. Linda wasn't a hermit; hers was the sort of shyness that dissolved in a crowd. What she hated was to be seen in her own habitat, among her own things, the nest she'd built around her. Soon after that meeting she finally sold the house in Swampscott and rented a room from a colleague at the high school. Then she moved to Nahant. Then, once retired, to an apartment in Melrose, and finally to a studio in a converted elementary school in Waltham. Jack was invited to none of these places. Perhaps she was trying to throw him off her trail. He couldn't even remember whose idea it had been, that disastrous first visit.

Had he said, *Why don't you bring me home to meet your mother*? Had Sadie said, *Sure, no big deal, we'll just go to the house, we'll go to the place where my father died, and you'll meet my mother, and we'll all be happy*?

Ever after, Jack worked on winning Linda over. Mostly he succeeded. He needed a role for those times. He was not her child: What was more grotesque than that American trampling of boundaries, calling your in-laws Mom and Dad, *I haven't lost a daughter, I've gained a son*, that whiff of incest and separation at birth? Nor was he a replacement husband, a tinkerer, an offered elbow at the opera, *Aren't I lucky to have two such beautiful dates*: that was just as disgusting. He wasn't a friend, though he grew to love Linda Brody decorously— a business relationship, a fond one, a banker or butler. A trusted member of staff.

Of the three of them, only Sadie worked year-round, as an editor for a numismatic magazine (her father had been a coin collector, a biographical detail that had landed her the job). After grad school Jack had lucked into a visiting position at Boston University, then a permanent one. Summers he accompanied Linda to games at Fenway—for her sake, he'd affected an interest in baseball, which eventually became genuine, he would have thought lifelong but then the Red Sox broke his heart by becoming successful, not once but over and over. He learned the secret of Linda, perhaps of all in-laws, which was to fold his own personality in half, and quarters, and eighths, then tuck it into his pocket. He allowed himself to be lectured; he offered himself up as the brunt of jokes. The widow Brody. Baseball, museums, movies, but Sadie was what they had in common, though they did not speak of her. They both respected her privacy.

Sadie'd been so little when her father died, an only child. A freak accident, she told Jack once. Did she want to talk about it? She did not. He thought he'd be the sort of person in a marriage—they weren't married yet—to whom anything might be told. That was true of the small stuff, the nutshell jealousies, the unusual rashes on inner thighs, the basest functions of the body and the psyche. Not the big things. She had one picture of her father looking toweringly tall, a sort of diamond-shaped monolith, wider at the beltline than anywhere else. He smiled, showed off his bad teeth.

Sometimes Jack thought that if only he could solve the riddle of Timothy Brody he could go forward in life. They'd get married. Have a kid. They were waiting for a sign. As though they would follow a sign. As though they'd be able to read it.

In July of his twelfth year with Sadie, Jack answered the phone to hear a man with a thick Boston accent say, "Is that Jack? I'm a friend of Linda." *Linder.* "She could use your help. She took a tumble."

Jack could hear Linda in the background saying, "Tell him I'm fine!"

"She's fallen down?"

"She's just in a bit of a pickle. Could you come over to her place?"

"Sure," he said. "Let me just call—"

"She says don't bother Sadie," said the voice. In a stage whisper he said, "She's embarrassed."

"I'll be right over. But—can you tell me the address?"

He didn't tell the voice that he couldn't drive; he grabbed a cab. It was hot in Boston, the kind of heat he resented. Linda's building was called the Schoolhouse, which sounded picturesque but was only accurate: twenty apartments, some with blackboards and some with tiny porcelain water fountains. His cell phone sat in his pocket, accusing him of treachery. He should call Sadie. It was Sadie to whom he was bound.

He rang the bell by the front door and was buzzed in without having to explain himself. The hallways were air-conditioned. Sadie had been enchanted by the Schoolhouse when she visited her mother, but Jack knew that no place once devoted to the education of children is enchanted without also being haunted. He could smell, quite suddenly, gym class. Not kindergarten gym class—cinnamon toast, artificial fruit, the squeals of five-year-olds allowed to run at top speed—but sixth grade. Half the girls budding, three or four in full bloody bloom. Boys, too, with wobbly chubby tummies and weak arms. The smell of burning flesh: thighs on climbing ropes, knees on the floor, what Jack would have called Indian burns. Maybe they still called them that. Lunch: square pizza, pickly tuna salad. Smoke from the teachers' lounge. Turning a school into a residence, thought Jack, was as bad as building your home on top of a cemetery.

Linda's door was marked PRINCIPAL in black paint on chicken-wired glass. A short, fat man of Linda's age in a baby blue polo shirt opened it.

"Hey! Come in, Professor. I'm Arturo. Vitale. You're the son-in-law."

"Not officially."

"No kidding? You're not married? I got the idea you were married."

They went down a little corridor into the apartment, four long windows letting in four tranches of sunlight, exposed brick, a kitchen in the corner, handsome green-shaded lights hanging from the ceiling, and, in the middle of the floor, Linda Brody, leaning on a wooden chair. She held a cloth to her head. She was surrounded by boxes, though she'd lived here awhile. Was she moving out? Were the boxes permanent? Jack felt as though he were the one who'd been in the accident, hit by a truck and pushed through miles and walls to end up here. In the years he'd known her, she'd aged very little, but now she looked ancient with worry. Her floral dress was hiked up. He could see too much of her legs.

"Not married yet," Linda said.

"Not yet," agreed Jack. He knelt down next to her and surreptitiously pulled down her skirt. "Linda," he said, "what's going on?"

"Well, I feel *stupid*," said Linda. She took the cloth away from her temple and regarded the pink streak left behind. There was a matching streak in her hair. "I'm not sure what's happened."

"Took a tumble," said Arturo, squatting down.

Jack looked at him. "Why isn't she at a hospital?"

"She said, don't want to go. Hey, maybe me and Lindy will beat you two to the altar."

"We're not getting married," Linda told Jack.

"You don't know," said Arturo. "Who can predict the vicissitudes of life?"

Linda frowned, put the cloth back, and Jack touched his own head. His brain felt injured; he wanted somebody else to take charge of the situation, load him onto a litter. The boxes around her were filled with items wrapped in newspaper.

"Are you moving again?" he asked.

"No. Just putting things in order."

"Selling some stuff off, hopefully," said Arturo.

"Who *are* you," Jack asked, and Linda answered for him: "Antique dealer. Old friend. Do you think you can help me get to my feet?"

"Shoulder," said Arturo, pointing.

The arm that wasn't holding the cloth to her head dangled, as though she had no shoulder at all.

"Bet any amount of money that's dislocated," said Arturo. "Head, shoulder, let's don't touch her."

"Linda," said Jack. He couldn't stand to look at the wrongness of arm. "I'm going to call an ambulance. Then I'm going to call Sadie."

After a moment Linda said, "If you must, call the ambulance."

"For the record," said Arturo, "I wanted to call both."

What *record*?

"Sadie's terrible in situations like this," said Linda.

"Is she?"

"Tell her afterward, when I'm all patched up and home."

"You don't think that will hurt her feelings?"

"Tough if it does," said Linda. "I mean, maybe. Jack, don't

call her. I know you think I spoil her, but—of course, you understand, you were basically an only child yourself. Sadie told me—what with your sisters grown and out of the house, I'm sure your parents coddled you."

He was thirty-six years old and had never been coddled a day in his life. Even when he went out with Linda, he paid for everything: the movie tickets, the museum admissions, the garlic soups and strong coffees at Café Pamplona.

"All right," said Jack.

Arturo squatted by one of the boxes, knees apart to give his stomach room. "I called nine-one-one." Then he pulled a newspaper-wrapped lump from a box. "Might as well, while we're waiting." Inside was a blue-and-white vase with twisted handles, a scowling profile painted on one side— Breton, Jack knew. He'd grown up with pottery like it, though nothing so fine as this. That old notion: a thing of beauty. Jack wanted it.

"Tim had good taste," said Arturo to Linda.

"*That* thing," said Linda. "I haven't seen it in years. Plenty more like it, from what I remember."

The EMTs rang the bell then came with their stretcher down the corridor, three bland young people, all with lank ponytails. "What did you *do*, Linda?" one shouted at her. Another said, "This place is *cute*."

"It's not cute," said Linda. They lifted her to the stretcher.

"It's cute," said Arturo, "you're cute, it's very cute."

"I'm a grown woman," said Linda, rolling out the door.

"For sure," said Arturo. "And now you live in a school-house, in the principal's office, like a storybook mouse."

Once they'd taken her away, Arturo said to Jack, "Come on. I'll drive you to the hospital. Where you from? You got a little accent."

"Upstate New York," he said.

Arturo had a set of keys; he locked the front door. "Oh. I thought Linda said you were British. Look at the bubblers!" he said, coming down the hall. He tried to operate one of the low water fountains with his foot.

In his mind Jack saw first Linda's shoulder, then the Breton vase, then all the boxes around, then Sadie. "What's she doing with all those boxes?"

"Unburdening herself?" said Arturo, elbowing open the Schoolhouse's front door. "Past twenty years she's had them in storage. When Tim died she just—packed 'em away. She's been paying monthly ever since. Crazy. Here you go." Arturo unlocked the passenger side of a pristine old Mercedes-Benz. Jack had imagined a piece-of-shit car, filled with old books. "It's all her husband's stuff. I think she thought she and the kid would move. You know he died in that house. Somehow, they got stuck. Stuck in Swampscott. Nice girl."

"Sadie? She is."

"I'm not asking you she's a nice girl, I'm telling you: she's a nice girl."

"You've met her."

"I knew her when she was a kid. Lived across from them in Swampscott. I did see her awhile, Linda, till she moved away, another thing don't tell Sadie. Last week she—Linda—called me up to say she's clearing out the storage, did I want to look at some of Tim's stuff, I say sure, why not. Mostly I deal in prints, but you know: overlap. Newton-Wellesley's up this way?"

"I don't know."

"You don't know a lot," said Arturo.

Inside the ER, Jack was trying to orient himself when he heard what he understood, though he had never heard it before, was Linda making a long animal noise of pain: a bay, a caterwaul. It did not sound like something you could live through. Instinctively he began to run, toward the source of pain or past it. The little area where he expected to find her had been closed up with blue-gray curtains. He stood outside of it trembling, and then one medical professional drew the curtains and another stepped out, and there was Linda, forehead spangled with sweat.

"Ah," she said, "that's better. They put my shoulder right. Arturo knew what he was talking about. You shouldn't have bet him."

"I didn't bet him. Jesus."

"They call it reducing a shoulder," said Linda.

Because of the head injury they wanted to keep her overnight; they wanted to keep an eye on her foot, too. She would stay in the ER till a bed was found on some distant floor.

"A bother," she said.

"You're not a bother."

She said, "I need to ask you something."

"Sure."

"Sadie was nine when her father died."

"That's a bad age," said Jack, trying to sound sage and empathetic.

"They're all bad ages," said Linda. "Let's not rank them. I have a friend who says, if you lose a parent early, there is part of you that stays that age forever. And of course it's worse for Sadie. Because of the trauma. Of being there."

"Oh," said Jack.

"She saw her father die. You know that."

He did not, but he couldn't say so. "Yes," he said. Then, "I will."

"Will what?"

"Look after Sadie."

"Not after Sadie," said Linda. "Me. I don't know that she could do it, worst comes to worst. Your parents have all those daughters, so I don't feel too bad about asking. Will you?"

"Yes," he said.

"Don't worry too much," said Linda, though he was already worried and planned to worry for the foreseeable future. "I have every intention of dying in my sleep."

Then there Sadie was, in a linen jumpsuit against the heat, billowing and flowered and wrong for her, beige and bright yellow—who would put an empire waist on a jumpsuit?—and they both loved her so dearly in it. She'd taken the afternoon to get a haircut, an old-fashioned bob when all the other hair of Greater Boston was pulled back into ponytails that day, or shorn into buzz cuts.

"Mom!" she said. "How are you?" She went to the opposite side of the bed.

"Furious, you want to know. I told Jack not to call you."

"He didn't. Arturo Vitale called me, that weirdo. What's going on?"

"Tripped over a box and now they want to do surgery on my foot, if you can imagine such a stupid thing."

"Well, I guess you should get surgery," said Sadie. "Good grief."

"They wanted to put some stitches in my scalp, but I said no." Linda touched her hair. "Most things they offer in hospitals you don't really have to do."

The dog in Jack wanted to leap over the bed. He wanted to find somebody in the hospital to marry them—there must be a chaplain, people were always getting married this close to mortality, though Linda was fine: she would live through this and go back to her storybook apartment, or so they thought. Everything seemed fine then. Everything seemed absolutely ordinary, Sadie in her terrible jumpsuit with the empire waist, looking like an ottoman, Linda intact. He stayed where he was. He didn't leap.

Later, as Sadie drove them home, he said, because there was no right question, "You saw your father die."

"My mother told you that."

"It's not true?"

"No, it's—I mean, it is true."

"Oh, honey," he said, because it was a moment for endearments though they never used endearments. Her new haircut matched her Weimar Republic eyebrows, the thin lines she'd plucked them into years ago, expecting that they'd grow back. Her lipstick was red. It suited her. It was only from the neck down that she looked clownish.

"Oh, honey," she repeated. *"That's* why I didn't tell you. He had an aneurysm."

"I'm sorry," he said. "Not a freak accident."

"I never said a freak accident."

He was sure she had—

"A freak *thing*," she said. "A freak thing."

———

Her father was crinkle-faced with bad teeth; he wore short-sleeved polyester shirts with black neckties; she loved him. He liked to show her card tricks. He was showing her one when he died.

"Look," he'd said. "There were once four thieves, and they decided to rob a department store." Jack of Clubs, Jack of Diamonds, Jack of Spades, Jack of Hearts. "And they landed their helicopter on the roof of the building." He put the jacks on the top of the deck of cards.

She was sitting in her bed, a little white Eastlake bed frame he'd found at a yard sale, such a long narrow shape they'd had to have a mattress made for it.

"The first thief went to the basement, fine china," he said, pulling a card from the top and inserting it in near the bottom. "The second, to the ground floor, perfume." Another card. "Third, lingerie. Fourth, jewelry. Then they heard the police outside, and they ran up—"

At this he riffled the cards but lost control of them. They flew into the air, then he himself folded up: he fell to his knees, as though surrendering to the imaginary playing card police force, he sat, he had a dopey expression on his face, he leaned back against the wall and closed his eyes, and his hands made funny giving-up gestures. She had laughed. Her father was very funny. Look at his hands, *I give up, I give up*.

That was the thing about her father's death, what she never told anyone, that she had thought it was a joke. It was not the sort of secret that explained everything, or even anything, though she knew that was what Jack believed: a key for a lock. Something architecturally essential that couldn't be disturbed without the help of professionals. A spell of the Snow White variety that might awaken her to a different life. Better? Worse? Probably not worth the risk. Maybe the beast preferred being a beast, the swan brothers the power of flight, the boy kidnapped by the Snow Queen the ability not to care about the feelings of others and also the luminous cold.

A knot on a vital net. An undiscovered organ. A tumor left alone for fear of rupture.

None of these. It was merely a thing that belonged to her.

There was a certain emotion that she'd felt, when she was looking at her father, thinking it was a joke, then understanding it wasn't, but not knowing yet the right response, what this meant for the rest of her life. Not shame: she'd hate for anyone to think that. Not sorrow, though sorrow was nearby. It was an emotion she'd never felt before and never would again, close to a religious conversion: deep certainty over a mystery. She couldn't bear another's interpretation. Couldn't imagine converting any of it into words. The memory—not of the facts of her father's death but of this

one moment—was hers, only hers, like one of those morbid Victorian lockets with a dead beloved's woven hair. How
strange, to use the dead matter of a person's head to stand in
for all of a dead person. How right, too. Put it behind glass.
String it on a chain. Wear it close to your heart. Don't submit
it to anyone else's unraveling.

ROBINSON CRUSOE AT
THE WATERPARK

They had come to Galveston, the boy and his fathers, to look at the ocean and chaw on saltwater taffy, but Galveston was solid November fog. As they drove down Seawall Boulevard, the Pleasure Pier emerged from the mist like a ghost ship: first the multicolored lights of the roller coaster and Ferris wheel, then a billboard for a restaurant: BUBBA GUMP SHRIMP CO.

"Good God," said Bruno, the older father, the *old* one. The sky was mild as a milk-glass rabbit. He would have said this aloud, but nobody else in the car would know what milk glass was. Instead he tried, "I hate the seaside. Where are we going?"

"You know where," said Ernest, the younger father, who was driving.

Bruno had understood—when he fell in love with a young man, when they bought a house together, when he agreed to children (one child at least)—that his life would become narrower and deeper, fewer trips to Europe, more moments of surprising headlong love. He had never imagined that family life would mean this: a visit to an indoor German-themed waterpark in Galveston, Texas. The fog had done it. They were headed to a location called Schlitterbahn, where there was an artificial river, for their river-obsessed son.

"You'll feel at home," said Ernest consolingly. "Being German-themed yourself."

"Darling, I'm German-*flavored*. German-scented. Only my mother."

"A mother counts double," said Ernest.

Bruno inclined his head toward their son—born to a surrogate, with an anonymous donor egg—in the back seat. They had forbidden him video games, so the boy had fallen in thrall to a pocket calculator, which he carried everywhere, calculating nothing: he could count, reliably, to six. "Well," Bruno said.

"I mean, *your* mother," Ernest said. "Your particular mother."

But that was something Bruno and their son had in common. Bruno had an adoptive German-born mother, and a presumably English biological mother who had left him at a public library in Nottingham, England. Not in the book deposit, as he liked to claim, but in the ladies' room. In this way Bruno and the boy had the same mother: Anonymous. As in anthologies of poetry, she was the most prolific in human history. This particular Anonymous—Anonymous Nottingham—had left him behind like a beseeching letter to strangers; his parents had adopted him; his parents had divorced; his mother had brought him to America. That was his provenance. He cataloged manuscripts for an auction house in Houston, other people's beseeching letters, other people's diaries. Provenance was everything and nothing. The point was not to stay from whence you came, but to move along spectacularly and record every stop.

Still, he did hate the seaside. His beloved worked as a PR person for a technology company that specialized in something called *cloud services*, but Bruno was a person of paper, and the ocean was his enemy. The seaside turned books blowsy and loose. It threw sand everywhere. Its trashy restaurants left you blemished, oil-spotted. It drowned children, according to Bruno's mother. She had few fears, but drowning was one, and she had handed it down to her only son, like an ancestral christening gown that every generation must be photographed in.

The fog made them drive slowly, as though not to break their car upon it. Down on the beach a wedding party walked toward them: bride, groom, six blue-clad bridesmaids, two men in tuxes, all of them overweight, one whippet-thin photographer walking backward. In the lactic light they looked peculiarly buoyant on the sand. Above them, a line of large khaki birds flew parallel to the ocean, heads ducked to avoid the clouds.

"Pelicans!" said Ernest, then, in a hopeful, accusatory voice, "A wedding."

"Pelicans?" said Bruno. "Surely not." But there they were, single file and exact, military even, with the smug look of all pelicans. "Pelicans flock!"

"Well, sure," said Ernest. "What did you think?"

"I thought they were freelancers," said Bruno. "Pelicans!"

"They looked like brother and sister," said Ernest, "the bride and her groom. Like salt and pepper shakers."

"They did," said Bruno.

The three people in the car, on the other hand, looked nothing alike, though strangers could tell they belonged together. Strangers were always trying to perform the spiritual arithmetic: the tall paunchy goateed near–senior citizen, the short hirsute broad-shouldered young man, the otherworldly child, who called now, from the back seat, in his thrillingly husky voice, his dreams filled with artificial rivers, "Schlitterbomb!"

"*Bahn*," said Ernest, and Bruno said, "That's right, darling, Schlitterbomb."

Ernest and Bruno had not married, not legally and not, as Ernest would have liked, in a church, or in a friend's backyard, or on a beach. Bruno did not believe in weddings, though he'd been married once, once for fifteen years, to a woman. He'd been the young husband then. Now, when Ernest brought marriage up, Bruno said, "I'm an old hippie," which was true insofar that he, unlike Ernest, had been alive in the 1960s and had done some drugs.

Why marry, after all? The boy stirring in the back seat *was* their marriage, even though, from the start, it was Ernest who had summoned him up, first as a dream and then as a plan and then as a to-do list. It was Ernest who'd wanted a child, and then specified a biological one, who'd found the donor egg, and the surrogate, and then offered what he thought was a compromise: they could mix their sperm together. "Oh God, how revolting," said Bruno, and Ernest had pointed out gently that it wouldn't be exactly the first time.

"But not in a laboratory," said Bruno, who ordinarily was the one with a sense of humor. And so the boy was Ernest's child by blood, and Bruno's by legal adoption. Ernest was Daddy and Bruno was Pop; Ernest believed in vows, Bruno in facts and deeds. The important fact was four years old. The fact was named Cody. The fact had never-cut red hair that hung to his shoulders and was so fair-skinned as to be combustible. Every day he was slathered in sunscreen; the first freckle would be a tragedy Ernest might never recover from. God knew when they'd manage a first haircut. When Cody and Bruno were out in the world together, they were generally taken for grandfather and granddaughter, and this thorough wrongness incensed Ernest, though Bruno had learned over the years not to take the mistakes of others too seriously, not when his own mistakes required so much analysis. He couldn't explain to Ernest the real trouble with a wedding: Ernest's shocking taste, which he, Bruno, would have to go along with, and smile, and declare himself happy. "I like peach," Ernest would say, displaying a napkin. Or, "My family loves disco music." Or, "We could have beef Wellington."

Once upon a time, Bruno had had opinions about everything—the politics of Eastern Europe, baby clothes, how airline stewardesses should comport themselves, interior decoration. Then: Ernest. Ernest, from a happy Cuban-American family, had grown up going to Disney World for vacations and watching sports on television and buying clothing in actual shopping malls. Ernest had quite the worst taste Bruno had ever encountered. Up-to-date American taste. For instance: Bruno had never imagined that a person he loved could admire, never mind long for, the abomination that was an open-plan house. Proper houses had doors, had walls, had secrets. But as they watched real estate programs for tips on buying—neither had ever owned property, Ernest because he was young and Bruno because he was lazy—he was horrified to hear Ernest say, "Now see, that's perfect. You can see everything from the kitchen."

"Do you know who else likes to see everything from the kitchen?" Bruno asked. "The Devil. Hell is entirely without doors."

"Heaven doesn't *need* doors," said Ernest.

Then Bruno had to remind himself that Ernest actually believed in heaven and hell, at least a little. So he said of the interior decorator on the television, "Look at that fool. I'm to trust him to arrange my furniture when he can't even wear a hat at an appealing angle?" *Look at that fool, yes*, he thought to himself, of himself. That old fool would live in a panopticon, for love of Ernest.

And so Bruno decided to treat his opinions like a childhood collection—decorative spoons, matchbooks—something comprehensive and useless. Put it all away, beneath the bed. Let Ernest decide; let Bruno feel superior. Now they owned a house in Houston, Texas, where when you walked in the front door you could see the kitchen, the dishes in the sink, the nook with the small offering to the gods that was the child's breakfast: a stem end of baguette, split and spread with jam. The playroom, the backyard, all the ways you could bolt.

Bruno had given up a lot for Ernest. He would not tolerate a wedding.

Schlitterbahn was an enormous medical military arachnoid construction, candy-colored tube slides corkscrewing out of barracks. In the summer it was open to the air; in November, half the park was closed, and half was covered against the weather. Bruno had looked up details on his phone; now he said aloud the fake German names in the most authentic German accent he could conjure, the voice of his mother. "Blastenhoff," he said. "Wasserfest. Surfenburg."

No matter what you renounced in this life, fate would provide the parody. At the Schlitterbahn box office they had to offer their wrists, and in a quiet ceremony they were braceleted, married to the park. The outdoor attractions—that was the word, *attractions*—were closed, but there were plenty of indoor attractions. "Most of my own attractions have been indoors," said Bruno to the young officiant, a plump woman with calligraphed eyebrows, who brandished another bracelet and asked if they wanted splash cash. *Do we?* asked Bruno. *Yes*, said Ernest. He shifted Cody on his hip. The boy had already put on his orange goggles, and he rubbed like a robot cat against Ernest's ear. "Honey, ouch," said Ernest. "You take it, Gravy." He stepped aside so that Bruno could offer his wrist to the young woman a second time.

"I'm a good swimmer," the boy told her.

"Are you? That's great!"

"Well," said Bruno.

"I *am*," the boy insisted. The rule of the household was to encourage, but Bruno wanted to say, *No, sweetheart, you're an awful swimmer. You suck.* One of the things he hadn't realized before having a child: how many ways there were to die of self-confidence.

In the locker room they crammed their clothing into a minuscule cubby. Only in a bathing suit did Ernest seem un-American: dark, furred, in a pair of unfashionably short but devastating red swim trunks, a 1960s movie idol from another country. Not a Frankie or a Bobby—a Francesco, a Roberto. "Handsome," said Bruno, accusingly, but Ernest shook his head.

"Ah well," said Bruno, and started to pull on his navy swimming shirt.

"You don't need that," said Ernest. "It's all inside."

"*I* need it," said Bruno, touching his stomach. "What's so German about this place? Apart from the nonsensical names?"

"I want a river," said Cody, shivering in his lime-green tights—ankle-length, to protect him from the sun and cold both.

"And so you shall have one," said Bruno.

Bruno took one hand, Ernest the other. They could feel the current flow through their little conductor.

The boy and his rivers. At this, and only this, he was a prodigy. He was slow to walk, to talk, to eat solid food. He still wore a diaper at night, requested another diaper once a day to move his bowels, which he would only do in the kitchen, next to the cupboard with the lazy Susan. Bruno, according to his mother, had been entirely toilet-trained at one and a half, but Cody would be a kindergartener before the process was done. "It's the sign of a genius," said one of the mothers at preschool. "Coincidentally," Bruno had answered, "also the sign of an idiot." What the mother had meant was it could go either way; they were not yet at the fork in the road between *gifted* and *special*. But this mother had children who were toilet-trained at ordinary ages, who hit every milestone in excellent time. Modern parenthood: other parents examined your children for deficiencies so they could augur their own child's future from your child's psychic entrails.

They wandered down a Plexiglas corridor, in and out of the warmth that fell from the overhead heat lamps. At a dead end a gothicky arrow captioned with gothicky letters pointed right, to something called FAUST UND FURIOUS.

"He was German, wasn't he?" Ernest asked. "Faust?"

After a moment Bruno said, "*Tech*nically."

Eventually they found a room filled with children and their parents, a pirate ship run aground in a shallow pool, hordes of insufficiently dressed mortals. The variety of swimming costumes! Chubby women in two-piece suits, middle-aged women in waterproof dresses, men in flowered trunks, Speedos, ankle-length pants. And the navels: sinkholes, champagne corks, thumbprints. Bruno's own belly button was inward; so was Ernest's; the boy's a little love knot, a souvenir of the day he'd been delivered to them.

Children flew down slides and splash landed. Parents stood watching, or walked babies through the water, or lay on deck chairs as though sunbathing beneath the corrugated roof. Two lifeguards in pointless sunglasses wandered around mid-shin in the water, clutching long foam rescue devices to their abdomens.

The boy started to run in.

"Walking feet!" called Ernest. "Careful, honey." He turned to Bruno. "Was this a terrible idea?"

"This was your idea."

"We should get him a life jacket."

"It's one foot of water."

"You can drown in three inches."

"I know all the ways you can drown," said Bruno.

"Yes," said Ernest, "I'm sorry."

They looked back. The boy was already gone.

Dead, Bruno decided. He felt this any time he couldn't locate Cody for more than a minute, even in games of hide-and-go-seek, when the boy wouldn't answer his name: an absolute conviction that he was now looking for a corpse. This was something he had never told Ernest, who believed Bruno too laissez-faire to do any real parenting. Ernest was reasonable, logical, in his worry. He had a sense of proportion. For Bruno, there was nothing between uncertainty and catastrophe. That was his secret.

"Where is he," he asked Ernest now.

"He's somewhere—"

They ran sloshily through the water. Behind the pirate ship was a smaller slide shaped like a madcap gape-mouthed frog, and here they found the boy sliding down the frog's great tongue. The goggles gave him the look of a scientist testing gravity.

They perched on the edge of the pool and watched the frog as it vomited toddlers. Toddlers, and Cody, who went up the steps along the frog's spine and down its tongue as though practicing for later: that exactitude and joylessness. The air seemed made of screaming and flesh. Bruno was grateful for his swim shirt, which hid his gut. He had the urge to reach out with bent fingers and just brush the inside hem of Ernest's swim trunks, imperceptibly, though it wouldn't be imperceptible to Ernest, and Ernest wouldn't approve.

He did it anyhow.

"Gravy," said Ernest. But he hooked one pinky into Bruno's Schlitterbahn bracelet and gave it a fond tug.

Then Cody was at their knees. "I want my river," he said. "I want to tube on my river."

"Of course," said Bruno, and Cody smiled again. His teeth were even, loosely strung. Bruno had always been appalled by parents who lamented the passing of their children's youth. *If you could just keep them this age!* And what would be the result? A child like a bound foot, a bonsai tree.

O Cody and his milk teeth: just a little longer, please.

The fact was Bruno was no better than anyone: he knew they'd gotten the best one. The *best* child, the most beautiful and distinct. The red hair out of nowhere, the ability to hail a waitress across a restaurant. The love of maps, and of birds, the obsession with Charlie Chaplin. The native slapstick. The way he liked to caress with his shoulders and the side of his head. His animal nature. Yes, he loved birds but he wanted to take them out of the sky, too. Sometimes Bruno worried that this was an inheritance from him, how they both wanted everything they loved twitching under the weight of one big paw.

A pair of double doors took them outside into the chill, where a heated pool spun steam from its surface, as though it were the source of Galveston's fog, on one side a swim-up bar advertising Bud Light. A middle-aged woman sat on a half-sunk bar stool and tipped blue fluid into her mouth from a statuesque glass.

"A bar," said Ernest, in a voice of wonder, he who had given up bars for parenthood. (Bruno had given them up longer ago, for other reasons.)

"Have a drink," Bruno said.

"Really?"

"Why not? We're on vacation."

They stepped, the three of them, into the slapping heat of the pool. The bartender was a young man with dark skin and dreadlocks, perhaps hired to match the island theme. He was dry, the bar itself a dam that kept back the water. "Under eighteen's got to be on the other side," he said, in a Texan accent. He indicated a beaded rope stretched across the middle of the pool. "I'm sorry, y'all," he said.

"Oh well," said Ernest, turning around.

"Sit," said Bruno. "Shall we find the river, Code? While Daddy rests and has a drink."

"Yes," said Cody seriously, as though he'd been arguing this for hours.

"No," said Ernest.

"Have a margarita," said Bruno, who knew that to be granted permission was a kind of love for the long-partnered. Nothing major, not quitting your job to be an artist, not traveling solo for six months. A drink. Another slice of cake. An hour of foolish pleasure in bed with somebody else. The love of children was said to be unconditional, but it was nothing but conditions. *I don't love you anymore!* Cody might shout, when refused more television, and Ernest—the disciplinarian

and therefore the spurned—would say, *You don't mean it.*
But Bruno was a man of the world, Bruno could see that it
was exactly true, just as in another hour it would be exactly
false. That was the distressing thing about some people, how
their love was like the beaded rope across the pool: the sub-
stance was continuous, but it was only the beads that kept it
afloat. Some people could put love down and pick it back up
and not know why your feelings were hurt by the loveless
intervals, which in the end made no difference.

"Are you sure?" Ernest asked.

"What a nice grandpa!" said the lady at the bar. Her sun
hat appeared, like its owner, intoxicated but doing its best.

"Not really," said Bruno.

"I'm just being friendly," the woman said, in a menacing
voice.

"Me too," said Bruno. To Ernest, he said, "Sit and have a
drink. For God's sake, when were you last alone?"

Ernest took a seat around the corner from the woman,
who swiveled on her stool to watch him pass. "I won't know
what to do with myself," he said, and then shyly, gesturing
at Bruno's wrist, "You've got the money."

"Of course!" He waded back into the pool. "Stay there,
Cody."

"Cold," said Cody, and shivered dramatically. "Let's go to
the river."

"You're doing *great*," Bruno said warmly. "Now, how does
this work?"

The bartender took his wrist with a tender familiarity, a
secret handshake, a pulse-taking. Just in case Bruno hadn't

caught his meaning, the bartender winked, in a cousinly way. He moved Bruno's wrist past the register, which beeped.

"You could buy *me* a drink," said the woman. Her glass was empty; her teeth were blue. "It's Thanksgiving. It's Thanksgiving *tomorrow*. I'm drunk."

"I know," said Bruno.

"Really?" said the woman.

"This isn't, as I believe we say, my first rodeo. And for the lady." He nodded at the bartender, but perhaps he only longed for another gentle handling of his wrist, the beep that acknowledged a transaction. There it was. "Magic!"

"There's a transponder," Ernest explained. "It keeps track."

"Cloud services," said Bruno.

"I don't think so," said the bartender.

"Cloud services," said Bruno, more seriously, and Ernest said, "Yes."

Back inside, around the corner, some poor soul in a dachshund costume talked—no, silently communed—with a tube-topped woman and her crewcutted preteen son. The dachshund costume wore a collar with a large round tag that said SCHATZIE! Its mouth was open in a hideous permanent smile, filled in with a black net grille. Behind the grille glittered a pair of human eyes. Bruno tried to meet them. It was as misbegotten a creature as Hieronymus Bosch ever dreamt up. Bruno and Cody turned onto a bridge, and looked over, and there it was: the river. Families floated along on single inner tubes, or on figure-eight-shaped inner tubes built for two. In Texas, *tube* was a verb, meaning, to ride upon one. The chlorinated air smelled of infection being held just at bay.

"River," said Cody.

The bridge led eventually to an artificial beach. The river was circular. On the right families pushed off on their journeys; on the left, they staggered out, pulling their inner tubes behind them. Bruno had the familiar sensation of having washed up himself on some shore, with no memory of his passage—not just how he got here, Schlitterbahn, Galveston, Texas, but his life, in which he lived with a man and had a child and loved both.

He found a double inner tube from a stack near the water, a doughnut on one side and on the other a ring with a plastic floor that said BABY SEAT. MAX WEIGHT 25 POUNDS. He had no idea how much the boy weighed. That was Ernest's department. Look at him, skinny thing, his rib cage an upturned rowboat. They waded in, and Bruno lifted Cody into the baby seat so he faced forward, could hold on to the handles on either side. They pushed out, and the current took them. Bruno heaved his torso up and grabbed the tube on either side of the boy. They went around a corner, past a palm tree and a flotilla of fully dressed women in hijabs floating together.

He had the panicky, recurring feeling that he'd forgotten to remove his watch, but it was only the shackles of the waterpark around his wrists. Half the people in the artificial river were swimming it, a whirl of limbs, no vessels. Boys, mostly, of all ethnicities, pink and umber and tawny and brown and sienna. It seemed as though there'd been a shipment of boys, and their boat had crashed, and here were the survivors. *The Raft of the Medusa* at the Waterpark. There were a lot of them, shouting in petrifying pleasure at one another. The water got rougher. Bruno tightened his grip on the rings. "Are you all right?" No answer. He realized with alarm that this had been a rotten idea. Impossible to know how deep the water was. Deep enough to buffet them along. A baby seat? Who would take a baby on something like this? They ran over one of the swimming boys, who popped up choking, laughing.

Bruno knew all the ways you could drown because his mother had told him, and because of Eleanor, now ten years dead, his wife for fifteen years, Eleanor of the psychiatrists and misdiagnoses, Eleanor whom he loved as well as he'd ever imagined loving anyone, until he met Ernest, when he realized his essential trouble might also have been a question of extraordinary misdiagnosis, though he only had himself to blame.

Eleanor, had she been alive, would have made fun of Ernest, not because he was a man (which might have thrilled her) but because he was *conventional.* A terrible insult, from Eleanor. To not know Faust was the fiction and Goethe the German! They had never had children because she had a horror of a living thing inside her body; she said she couldn't believe that modern science hadn't figured out a less barbaric way to reproduce. One that might allow you to drink as much as you liked, for instance: the studies were just coming out, then, suggesting in utero alcohol was a bad idea. (So why, he imagined her saying now, surveying the Schlitterbahn crowds, did children ever since seem to be getting *stupider*?) She was the author of most of Bruno's opinions. Holding them was his way of keeping her alive; not insisting on them was his way of doing the same for himself. She had started to lose her memory. *Could be early Alzheimer's,* her doctor said, *or arteriosclerosis, or more likely alcoholic insult to the brain*, and Bruno hadn't cared: you don't worry about arson or faulty wiring till *after* the structure has fully burned to the ground. She'd died in the swimming pool at their apartment complex, drowned, full of vodka and valium, she who'd once swum laps for an hour every morning. Maybe she'd forgotten how many pills she'd taken. Maybe she'd merely remembered the full measure of what she'd lost. *You must have known*, said Ernest, when they fell in love a year later, *you knew all along about yourself, you liked men.* Bruno could only say, *I was waiting for you.*

He and Eleanor had been married in a sad ritual. Her parents were dead; his mother, who was only ten years older than Eleanor, had hated her immediately. Eleanor had bought a white dress, because Bruno had told her that his mother cared about such things. His mother had laughed in her face. "Well," said Eleanor, afterward, "we'll never do *that* again, thank God."

The current picked up. The banks of the river were made of tile. The palisades were tiled as well, and studded with more bored lifeguards, standing like unemployed goats. He looked up and longed for the pelicans of the morning, their competence and precision. His biceps ached from holding on. He couldn't see Cody's face. At the next turn, a young park employee stood up to his waist in the crashing water. His job was to catch inner tubes as they threatened to bash into a wall, to send them in the right direction. How could so badly designed a thing exist at a place meant for children? Bruno paddled his feet. He wanted to avoid the guy, but instead they knocked right into him. "Sorry!" he shouted, and then they were shoved away, in the opposite direction, in front of the wave machine.

Now they were surrounded by loose boys and empty bobbing inner tubes. "Hold tight!" he commanded Cody, as he heard a wave behind them. A woman in a neon pink swimming dress clung to a single inner tube. Clawed at it. They hadn't seen this stretch of river from the bridge. Every few seconds some hidden mechanism slapped out a wave, which then lifted the flotsam—people, tubes, goggles, swim shoes—and dropped the flotsam, and smacked the flotsam on the head. *Even artificial rivers are careless, Cody.*

Survivors of the Whaleship *Essex* at the Waterpark. The *Lusitania* at the Waterpark. *The Poseidon Adventure* at the Waterpark.

He'd thought he hadn't wanted children because Eleanor hadn't wanted them. He *hadn't* wanted them for that reason. Eleanor was already forty when they'd married and she'd convinced herself she was too old. Perhaps he was too old, too, but here was his heartbreaker, screaming as they bounced along.

"Are you all right?"

The boy nodded the back of his head. You could hear the waves from the wave machine behind you before they lifted you up. That was good. They were just one turn from the beach. Now Bruno was holding Cody's right wrist to the starboard handle of the inner tube. Every wave threatened to scupper them. What would happen then? Would it jolt a lifeguard into action? Would the boy be picked up by the passengers of another tube? Sucked into the filtration system? Bruno thought of Ernest drinking at the swim-up bar,

Ernest who would never forgive himself, though he would forgive Bruno, and that would be the worst thing that could ever happen to either one of them. No, not the worst thing.

A bullying wave pushed the edge of their raft, tipped them, rushed overhead, and swept Cody away.

Above the river the burghers of Schlitterbahn saw the flash of pale flesh, the hair that streamed behind as though a cephalopodic defense, *Stay away*. The last inhabitant of the lost city of Atlantis, washed into the waters of Torrent River—that was its name. A little boy, surrounded and then eclipsed by the bigger boys, the wild boys of the German-themed waterpark. "Look out!" shouted a blue-tongued woman from the bridge, but she was drunk, and already the other people doubted what they had seen, and besides, so what? Those feral boys would take him in. They never went home, those boys; they lived here, they circled and circled, howling and laughing and dreaming of home.

"Cody!" Bruno shouted. "Cody!"

The boys found the body, and lifted it up, and then there was his own child's stunned face, one hand out, and Bruno snagged it, and they were back in each other's arms, bumping up onto the incline of the concrete beach. Cody coughed. He was alive. Not a lifeguard had shifted. They were surrounded by wild delight, shrieking, flesh, stove by a whale, but safe.

When they had staggered out—not onto dry land; there was nothing, nothing, nothing dry in all of Schlitterbahn—Bruno realized that the water had stripped the swimming tights right off, that Cody now stood naked, just as God had made him—though God hadn't been anywhere near Cody's conception, an event Ernest called a miracle. Quite the opposite, Bruno had thought. Ordinarily he hated God getting credit for Science's good work. Yet here the boy was, the narrow naked awkward miracle.

"Jesus," said a voice. A man, this new model they now made, tremendously fat from the hips up, an epidermic barrel, skinny as a kid from the hips down, such a precarious construction it hurt Bruno to look at him. "Cover that kid up!"

Their towels were back by the pirate ship. Bruno took off his shirt and draped it over his son to make him decent.

At the Wasserfest bar, Ernest stirred the slush at the bottom of his drink. O Schlitterbahn! The freckled, the fat, the hairy, the veiny, the chubby girls in bikinis, the umbilically pierced, the expertly tattooed, the amateurishly scrawled on, the comely, the grotesque, all the Boolean overlap: Ernest thought he'd never felt so tender to the variety of human bodies. He loved them all. Every bathing suit was an act of bravery.

"Yes," he said, to the bartender, whose name was Romeo, "I'd like another," and there was his family: Bruno with water dripping from his beard, Cody wrapped in some black cape, which he now flung off, saying, "Daddy! Daddy! I capsized! I capsized! I was saved!"

"You're naked!"

"Naked!" said Cody.

"Marry me," said Bruno, galumphing in.

A WALK-THROUGH
HUMAN HEART

Some grackles might possess souls and some grackles might possess intelligence but it was impossible to believe that any one grackle possessed both: not enough room in their brilliantined heads. A klatch of them walked unnervingly around the parking lot outside the vintage store like a family at a hotel wedding, looking for the right ballroom. One grackle was missing a foot, and Thea blamed him for it. If they had been magpies, she might have counted them up, wondering what they foretold, but grackles were just seagulls in widows' weeds. They weren't omens of anything except more grackles.

She was here to buy a present. The world had promised a baby (though the world broke such promises all the time), and Thea planned to become that uninteresting thing, a doting grandmother. What *was* doting? A sort of avian love, an affectionate pecking. Thea had already referred to the baby as *my baby*, and Georgia—who lived in Portland, where she'd grown up and nearly died—said, "Mom, don't be disgusting."

"Sorry," Thea had said. "Comes naturally. You're okay? You're taking care of yourself?"

"Martine's taking care of me."

"She should. But also—"

"I'm fine. I've been fine a long time. Hey, you know who I saw? Florence. At the farmers market. In some weird floral dress. Muumuu, I guess. She's old now. She got old."

"Well, she would have," said Thea. "That's just math."

She had not thought of Florence in years in the way she had not thought of furniture, or pavement, or the earth.

The vintage store was a cavern built of confiscated things. Immediately Thea's hatred of castoffery came upon her like an allergy. She wanted to sneeze with depression: all the fingerprinted objects that had made it just this far. Instead of stalactites overhead, a series of old suitcases hanging from hooks (flowered, plaid, their insufficient metal wheels exposed). Instead of stalagmites, the kind of bar stools once favored by kicky grandmothers.

She wouldn't be a *kicky* grandmother. If anybody indeed was kicky these days. Her apartment was so spare, people asked her when she had moved in though it had been ten years. Florence—her long-lost friend, lost on purpose, currently muumuued Florence—might be kicky by now, but she couldn't be a grandmother: her child was dead. That was only one difference between them, the one that counted.

Now Thea closed her eyes and envisioned the particular doll she wanted to buy. Was she trying to divine its presence or magic it into place? She pictured a baby doll amid the shot glasses and quilted skirts. Then she opened her eyes to the great accumulation.

No surprise that the memorabilia of her childhood was for sale—little plastic homunculi on rhomboid plinths inscribed I LOVE YOU THIS MUCH; Playboy drinking glasses; a lacy and emphatic Cross Your Heart bra. Her childhood was as ugly arranged by color and category as it had been in the kitchens and rumpus rooms and Spencers Gifts of her hometown. Wheat-patterned, avocado-hued: vintage. That's how it worked. Your belongings marched alongside you, as you moved toward death: thrift shop, vintage shop, antique store, museum. Look, Thea's chrome childhood bread box, with the Bakelite latch and the identifying badge: BREAD.

Behind the front counter, a woman in a strapless plaid dress shot through with gold stood sorting through a parliament of macramé owls. The owls smelled, no doubt, of tuna noodle casserole and Virginia Slims.

Thea leaned on the counter. The woman turned, holding a beige owl by its top and bottom, like a town crier with a proclamation. She was plump, luscious, with cat's-eye glasses, carmine lipstick, tattooed wings spread across the territory below her throat and above her breasts, her cleavage creasing the bottom. Her hair was the red pistachios used to be. "Something you're looking for?" she asked Thea.

"Yes," said Thea, and got shy. "Do you have a doll section?"

"Not really. I think we got a Pee-wee Herman. Or there's her." She pointed to a trepanned bisque head in the display case. "Other than that—not really. Here." The woman grabbed a photocopied brochure of local vintage shops and circled a number on a map. Soon she would age out of those glasses, or out of the implicit irony: she would be an actual middle-aged broad, not a young woman playing the part. "Try here. Amanda. On Burnett. She's got a ton of dolls."

All grackles were beautiful the way all babies were: if you liked them, yes. Otherwise, only an occasional specimen. They were not hummingbirds or cardinals; they did not flash. Sunlight revealed the iridescence in their dark plumage like poison in a glass. In the morning and evening, they held meetings on telephone wires: you drove under conventions of grackles, their shadowy bodies, their long pensive tails. The birds of Portland, Oregon, had wanted nothing from Thea except her dropped crumbs, which they busied away all busboy-like. In Austin, on the lawns of bungalows, grackles had a patient, dangerous, purposeful look. They seemed to *walk* more than most birds. Outside the vintage shop, the one-footed grackle hopped along the concrete blocks. His mouth was jacked open. He eyed Thea: *I'm a bird, but I could fuck you up.*

Thea had been a young mother and Florence an old one. They had brought their children to the same eurythmic dance class, Georgia because she was clumsy and Orly because he was graceful. The class was taught in a converted fire station by a Hawaiian woman the size of an eleven-year-old; she skipped and hit a round drum, followed by her dazzled students. There was a plate-glass window parents could spy through. "Make yourself a butterfly!" said the teacher. Georgia, age three, made herself a disgruntled Quasimodo with sciatica.

Her leotard was too big and gapped around her legs, and Thea loved her entirely. "Which one's yours?" Florence asked, and Thea pointed, said defensively, "I couldn't skip to save my life," and Florence said, "Chances are it won't come to that." Her own child, Orly, wore a little blue jumpsuit, like Jack LaLanne's but mid–chubby thigh, and even when the class was led in "Head, Shoulders, Knees, and Toes," Orly somehow did it *expressively*. He was an olive-skinned child with dark curly hair. Georgia was skinny and pale and freckled. Both of them three, but Thea was in her mid-twenties, and Florence somewhere in her forties. Old enough to be—

"Don't say it," said Florence, who in those days—on *that* day—wore striped dungarees and a sheer Indian shirt. Flowered, like the rumored muumuu. Altogether she seemed highly patterned, light blue eyes with navy blue flecks, a large nose with vertical creases at the bridge. Florence was happily married then to a lean professor of philosophy named Loren; Thea to Max, she thought also happily. If Thea tried—if she tried *now*, in Austin, Texas—she could conjure them up. The children, not the husbands; the husbands never met. Orly and Georgia, Georgia stumble skipping and Orly dancing. Beautiful children. That's what Florence said that first day, as they watched the class: she turned to Thea and said, "Wouldn't it be awful not to have beautiful children?"

The doll Thea sought was Baby Alive. You fed Baby Alive's mechanical mouth, and Baby Alive's mechanical digestive tract eventually emptied its mechanical bowels into its diaper, which you changed. *Please*, Georgia had said when she was eight, in the stunned weeping voice of a child whose parents didn't understand her passion, *peh-lease*. "You've got a baby doll," Thea had told her. "Pretend *it* can eat." Just a year ago, at her wedding to Martine, Georgia had mentioned the doll, and Thea had said, "Oh, if you'd really bugged me I would have gotten it for you," and Georgia had gasped, betrayed.

Thea couldn't buy anything for the baby until after the birth, for fear of attracting the evil eye, but she could buy the doll for Georgia. Georgia would find it touching, or she'd be hurt. Thea wasn't sure which reaction she hoped for. She knew her maternal love would always be edged with meanness, so as to matter: sometimes you needed a blade to get results.

Of Orly, Florence said, "Frankly, I worship that boy." Thea thought it was a funny way to feel about your own child. You worried about your kid; you loved her; you wondered what her existence said about you. Florence's adoration of Orly would have been intolerable had she not genuinely loved all children.

"I *worship* him," said Florence, "and you worship Georgia. Geor-jah," Florence called, and then said it again, the syllables distinct, cherry-dark and cherry-sweet.

"Hello," said Georgia.

Florence said, as though just remembering, "I think there might be cake."

They were sitting in Florence's kitchen, the children cross-legged on the floor eating canned spaghetti, the mothers at the table eating pumpernickel bread and salted butter.

The amiable Loren had baked the bread himself. At the mention of cake, Orly shut his eyes and rubbed his stomach. "Cake," he said. "Cake, cake, cake, cake." "Cake," Georgia agreed, though she regarded Orly with caution: he kept saying it like a toy machine gun—"Cakecakecakecakecake." She turned to her mother with a worried expression, a flutter of a smile, a private joke. *No*, thought Thea, *I do not worship her*. That would be immodest and unlucky. She worshipped no human being, except Florence herself, a little.

Every Saturday for two years, except summers, Thea and Georgia had lunch after dance with Florence and Orly in their house in Southeast Portland. The house had brown unpainted vertical siding, and looked like a hearty sport-related building somewhere in Europe: a sauna or ski chalet or the place where you strapped and unstrapped your ice skates at the edge of a frozen lake. It was the year that Thea's husband was finishing his dissertation, followed by the year that their marriage was breaking up.

After lunch, in the piney backyard, Orly would cartwheel or walk on his hands or spin until he fell down, and Georgia would somersault knock-kneed and askew, and they both ended up on their backs, laughing at the sky.

Then kindergarten, and Georgia was off to Meriwether Lewis and Orly to Woodstock, where he lasted a week.

"He bit his teacher," said Florence. "Mrs. Pietsch. I would have bit her, too."

But once you get used to biting, to expulsion, it's hard to stop. *He's a wonderful kid*, his teachers said, *but he bites*. Or: *He's wonderful, but he can't sit still*. Or: *He's a good kid. Come get your kid. You need to get your kid. I'm sorry*. Orly outgrew dance and he outgrew sports and he outgrew school. He outgrew his bed: he slept on his floor, in his closet, out in the world. In those years Thea heard from Florence only when he'd been missing awhile. "I was wondering if he'd called Georgia," said Florence. "He's always loved her so." He always *had* loved her, Thea said; he never had called. He went to rehab twice the year he was thirteen. Twinkle-eyed Vandyked Loren turned out to have a nineteenth-century streak to his parenthood, and Orly was sent for three months to a camp in Idaho for wayward boys. He came home furious, but with roses in his cheeks. He overdosed and detoxed five times before dying in the parking lot of the Safeway at sixteen, brought down to earth for good.

Perhaps he had died somewhere else and been brought there, the police said, as though that might be a solace.

The children weren't friends any longer, thank God. Fate and their mothers had kept them apart—Florence most of all. She decided that he was contagious—he must have caught his troubles from some other, worse boy—and this was the way she failed her son. Wasn't caution catching, too? Shouldn't he have been exposed to plenty of it?

That's what Thea guessed, anyhow.

The funeral was open casket, which surprised Thea. They'd combed the curls right out of his hair, though maybe he'd done that himself, alive; maybe they'd been working from a recent photo. On the church pew Thea and Georgia slid on the needlepointed cushions and did not know whether they were supposed to pray aloud with the believers or not. It was jam-packed. People wailed. You'd think the whole world would never recover.

Afterward, at the house, Florence held them by their elbows. How different did she look from the day they'd met thirteen years before at the converted fire station, the groovy mother, the mother of many colors? (How different would she look now, her child gone nearly that long?) This was the last time they might see each other, thought Thea. She wished she had *done* something, slept with Loren, loaned Orly money for his fatal dose, something that could not be forgiven. She didn't want Florence to come looking.

"He loved you," Florence said to Georgia, caressing her elbow, squeezing it.

"He loved everybody," said Georgia, who'd had to borrow a pair of her mother's pantyhose for the occasion.

"No," Florence said. "He loved you particularly."

Florence knew what she was doing. She was the sort of person, thought Thea, who said a thing aloud when she suspected it wasn't true. Not lying exactly, but as though she were wrestling with an immense and troublesome and essential emotion, and in telling you, gently, that it was a thing to be venerated, an unusual variety of love, she was handing you the corners so you could help gather. *He loved you particularly. You always loved each other.*

And then she let go, and Georgia was left holding that unwieldy feeling. It blew back over her, and she was caught.

She was sixteen. Not a prodigy at annihilation, like Orly, but a quick study.

The store on Burnett was not a mineral cave but an animal den, carved out by a creature partial to must and floral sheets and PEZ dispensers. A junk shop, a proper one, like walking into somebody else's disordered brain, which operated on this lie: it was good to collect ephemera because if things were worth saving—if a volume of Reader's Digest Condensed Books with abridgements of Ngaio Marsh could persist—why not all of us?

Thea peered into a display case full of drinking glasses that had once been jelly jars, with pictures of the Flintstones on them, another thing Georgia had begged for, and Thea could taste cloying grape on the crest of her tongue, bad jelly that you had to suffer through so you could drink later. They'd only ever gotten one, which Thea would have jettisoned when she'd left Portland. She had boxed up the board games and the stuffed animals, the decks of cards and bowling trophies, all of it now seemingly, eerily here, mangled and for sale.

The emptied rooms of dead children, she saw now. Or whose parents had given up on them. It wasn't really a store; it was too dense, too personal for that. A hoarding. Evidence of damage. You hoarded because you lost someone. Lost someone, and decided, *never again*, not a person, not a thing.

From the back room of the junk shop stepped the proprietress, a shopworn woman in her fifties with long knotted hair. The authoress of the hoarding. She wore gunmetal blue jeans and a plaid cowboy shirt with pearl snaps. Thea realized, with the feeling of a dropped package, that the woman must have been about her own age. It wasn't that Thea forgot she was fifty-two, only that people who were her own age were also fifty-two.

"Want something, darling?" the woman asked.

"I'm looking for a doll."

"We got dolls!"

"A particular kind," said Thea. "It was big in the seventies and eighties."

The woman covered her mouth, the way already quiet people do to listen, and nodded encouragingly.

"Baby Alive," said Thea.

The woman looked at Thea with a wet-eyed, accusing, marsupial expression. This went on for a while. It was like being on the phone with someone and not knowing whether you'd been disconnected. The longer Thea looked, the more varieties of emotion she detected: sorrow, fury, a tiny sense of humor trying to fill its sails with wind.

"If you don't—" said Thea at last.

The woman took her hand from her mouth. "Do," she said. "Think so. This way."

Longing always did bring you worse and worse places, to junk shops and deserted parks; longing had in Georgia's life taken her to unfamiliar dorm rooms when she was still in high school, to group houses and dingy apartments, to drink in, smoke in, shoot up in, and finally overdose, which she did for the first time in an abandoned house in East Portland. *First time*, that's what Florence called it when she phoned Thea. How had the news found her? But Thea was glad to hear Florence say, in the calm voice of a driver spinning into a ditch, "Here we go."

"Listen," said Florence. They were driving around the city. Georgia was locked up in rehab near Medford, but Florence was showing Thea the places she would need to look next time: the public parks, a particular arch under a particular bridge, the empty houses, the old communes gone off the rails. "You can't blame yourself, and you can't blame Georgia. She'll lie to you. I mean, obviously she's already lied to you, you know that. But she will lie and she'll steal. It's not her. It's the disease. It's out of her control. Your job is to love her. You have pills in the house? She'll steal them, and once she's stolen drugs she'll steal the next thing. That's what I've learned. Once your kid has done the first thing he'd never do there's nothing he *won't* do. Sorry. This is the truth. Sweet Georgia. I'm sorry. I just love that girl, we all do. Sometimes I think the mistake I made was I was too easy on him, and then I remember what he was like when he came back from Cullen—sorry, Idaho, the place we sent him—and then I think *that* was the mistake, that's what we couldn't come back from. I never wanted to send him there. It was Loren. He hit me once. Orly, I mean, Orly hit me. I don't think he ever remembered that he did that. In the ear. Thought he'd take it right off my head. You see this place? There's a group of kids? Goes all the way back. I've missed you, Thea. I'm sorry this is what's taken for you to call me. Nobody called me. Nobody. No, nobody. I had a kid everybody loved, and then he died, and where did that love go? Into outer space. Into other people's kids. I hope you know, Thea, that I will love you forever."

You could think a grackle was somebody you'd lost, or wronged, or owed a favor to, come back to settle accounts.

If Georgia, for instance, had not survived, Thea would have looked for evidence of her persistence everywhere. She would have kept everything, the board game called Life, the board game called Sorry!, the board game called Monopoly: Georgia's existence. Chinese checkers, and wept over the missing marbles, the empty dimples in the metal board.

"You," she might have said to a particular grackle. "Georgia. Is it?"

When Georgia got out of rehab, Thea took her to all her childhood favorite places: the ice cream parlor decorated like a nineteenth-century brothel, the mall skating rink, the walk-through heart at the science museum. Inside, you could hear it beat.

"Oh God," said Georgia in a voice of terror, touching the heart's wall. A ventricle hung over her head. "They should fill it with blood for the full effect."

"With cholesterol," said Thea. "Or heartbreak."

"With cocaine," said Georgia, then, "Do you think it beats all night long?"

"Yes," said Thea, but of course it was some man's job to turn it off at night, and on again in the morning. She pictured a mad scientist's horseshoe-shaped switch with a rubber handle on a wall.

Ka-thump, ka-thump. *We gotta get out of here*, she thought. Not the heart but the city. She'd already found the job in Austin when Georgia announced that, with money from her father, she would leave the country to clear her head. *To do what you want out of my sight*, thought Thea, who had assumed that Georgia would follow her to Texas, and Thea would never again have to drive around the neighborhoods of Georgia's disappearance, remembering *she might be in there* and *she might be dead*. That whole terrible night with Florence. But they'd both been wrong about Georgia.

Thea got rid of her house and everything in it. Burn the city to the ground, find the inflammable heart like a poet's in the ashes, wrap it in a handkerchief, bury it in a mausoleum beneath a mile of marble.

Love, love. The word meant nothing. They should replace it with another.

In the junk-shop back room, the woman scaled an outcropping of stacked record albums, covers scuffed to show the shape of the discs inside. Nearby was a box of thick seventy-eights, grackle black and grackle brilliant. Thea thought the cliff might come down. But the woman was goat-footed; she got to the top and came back down and handed over the doll.

Georgia, aged eight, had not just *wanted* Baby Alive: she had thought it would make *the difference*. What difference? The only one. Maybe it would have. It was hard to tell, ever, what would make it: the walk-through heart, the indulgent mother, the mean one. They'd driven into a ditch, then away.

They'd kept on going. They'd used up every bit of luck they had, making their getaway. Thea never spoke to Florence again, though Orly was still dead, would be dead forever.

And who's to say that's the order things happened in; was it only her junk-shop memory that had arranged them so? Maybe Orly had nothing to do with Georgia, child of divorce, always so uneasy in her body, made to take dance lessons because her mother wished her otherwise, and maybe it was Georgia who'd first pulled a plastic bag out of her pocket and waved it at Orly, Georgia who even now was vowing to raise her child differently: the baby would sleep in their bed, would have two mothers, two actual mothers, who planned to bend the world for their child instead of the easy other way around.

The doll was diaperless, and played with, and autographed: KITTY on its bicep. Its hair, like many an old lady's, had gone mauve with age.

"She's written on," said Thea, looking for a way out.

"Ballpoint." The woman spit on the tip of her finger and rubbed the *K* of *Kitty* away.

"Does it work?"

"Needs a battery, honey," the woman said, to the doll instead of Thea. She reached into her jeans pockets. "D or C," she mused, "D or C: D."

The doll had a hatch in her back, and the woman loaded a battery, flipped a switch, and turned the doll over.

The baby suckled at nothing. The woman lifted it to Thea, who put out her arms as though the baby were real. She took its churning weight. Instinctively she put her hand on the baby's chest to test for heartbeat, or breath, but could perceive only its mechanical hunger.

Could there have been a worse signal to the evil eye? Baby *Alive*? And what now? She could not take it home, but she could not leave it here. She couldn't turn it off, but she couldn't bear to see its empty mouth move and move. Maybe the TSA would see it in her suitcase and blow it up. She got to take her true love home all those years ago, and yes, she would dote on the new baby, but only because the baby would be a pinhole camera with which to look at her daughter, the near-total eclipse, the blinding event. She wanted to buy everything, the jelly jars and the PEZ dispensers, the never-played-with board games with the clicking spinners that told you how far to go and the cards that told you what you had to give up.

"I'll take her," Thea said. "Who else have you got?"

Look at the evening grackles strung on their overhead wires like Morse code! Impossible not to believe they spelled out something. But they didn't; they were meaningless, in their numbers and their prattle. The call of a grackle is known as a grackle: in the gloaming, the grackles grackle.

Maybe they *don't* want anything. Maybe they stare because they wonder what *you* signify. What brought you here, to their front lawn?

TWO SAD CLOWNS

Even Punch and Judy were in love once. They knew the exact clockwise adjustment required to fit their preposterous profiles together for a kiss, her nose to the left of his nose, his chin to the left of her chin. Before the slapstick and the swazzle, the crocodile and the constable, before above all the baby: they'd known how to be sweet to each other.

These people, too, Jack and Sadie. They'd met at a long-ago winter parade in Boston. Sadie had been walking home from a show at the Rat, drunk and heartbroken over nothing: twenty-one years old, the clamor of the smoky club still around her, a trailing cloud she imagined was visible. Her friends had terrible boyfriends, one after another, but she never did. When she felt particularly maudlin, she blamed it on her father's death when she was nine, though most of the time she thought that was neither here nor there. She liked to imagine him, the man who might love her. A performer of some kind, an actor or musician, somebody she could admire in the company of strangers. He'd have an accent and a death wish and depths of kindness. She wanted love so badly the longing felt like organ failure, but it was the longing itself that had rendered her unlovable, the way the starving are eventually unable to digest food. At the same time she believed she deserved love—not as much as anyone, but more. Only she would know what to do with it.

She was thinking of this, love and fantasy, as she came down Dartmouth toward Boylston and saw at the end of the block a claque of towering, angling, parading puppets, avalanche-faced, two stories high and neither male nor female. Their arms were operated by lumber, their mouths by levers. Some human fools followed behind with tambourines. Nobody whose mother ever truly loved them has ever taken pleasure in playing the tambourine.

By the time she got to Copley Square, the puppets had vanished. How was that possible? No, there was one, stretched out on the pavement alongside the public library. The parade had lost its spine, become a mob, but the downed puppet was away from that, one of its ears pressed to the ground and the other listening to God. Ordinarily she wasn't drawn to puppets. This one reminded her of a corpse at a wake. It demanded respect. Nobody loved it, either.

Its face was vast, the color of cartoon cheese. She went to its throat, then down its body to its hands, stacked one on the other; she touched a colossal thumb and felt the familiar consolation of papier-mâché. Its gray dress—habit? Cloak? What did you call the robes of a giant puppet?—lay flat on the ground as though bodiless. But it wasn't bodiless. From beneath the hem came a human man, tall and skeletal, Bakelite-eyed, exactly the sort of mortal a puppet might give birth to. His head was triangular, wide at the temples and narrow at the chin; his hair was dark marcel. He looked at her. She thought, *I might be the first woman he's ever met.* The expression on his face suggested this was possibly so. *A pup-peteer*, she thought. Yes. *Why not?*

Really Jack had renounced puppetry years ago, as a teenager. Tonight he was a mere volunteer who'd carried the puppet's train so that it wouldn't trail in the street. Still, many a man has improved because of mistaken identity. Been ru-ined, too.

She said, "I love puppets." In the bitter cold, her words turned white and lacey and lingered like doilies in the air. That was a form of ventriloquism, too.

"You don't," he said. "You fucking hate puppets."

He knew everything about her already, it seemed.

Later he would understand that love was a spotlight that had allowed him to perform, but at the moment it felt as though he'd become his true self: not a better person, but funnier and meaner. For now they headed to a bar down the street. The establishment had on its side a sign that said EATING DRINKING PIANO, though inside there was no piano and no food. He wasn't a puppeteer. He was a sort of Englishman, sort of American, who'd just gotten back from three years living in Exeter.

"Exeter, New Hampshire?" Sadie asked.

"Exeter, UK," he said. "What's Sadie short for?"

"Sadness," she answered.

The bar was a dream of a bar, ill lit and long, with people

in all the wooden booths. A precarity: it hung over the Mass Pike like a small-town rock formation—a stony profile, a balancing boulder—something that must be preserved at all costs. No dancing allowed. Any sudden movement might knock the bar into the turnpike. No jukebox. Never a band. In the ladies' room, you could pay a dime, press a plunger, and get misted with perfume.

"Bar stool?" he said, their first negotiation, but bar stools were made for long, lean fellows like him, not for women as short and squat as she. The bar stools were red-topped and trimmed with ribbed chrome.

"Let's see," she answered.

He gave her his hand. "Allow me."

The bartendress was a middle-aged woman with brown hair and auburn eyebrows and the oversized eyes of a cartoon deer. If she were a man they might have thought she looked like a cartoon wolf. She wore a bow tie and a skirt with suspenders. It was an era in America between fancy cocktails, before American pints of beer or decent glasses of wine in bars like EATING DRINKING PIANO.

"What'll you have?" the bartendress asked them.

"What'll I have indeed," said Jack. He tried to remember what you drank in America. "Gin and tonic."

"You?"

"Vodka soda with lime." She said to him, "My mother calls that the alcoholic's drink. Goes down easy and odorless."

"Are you?"

"No," she said, though if you'd known her then you wouldn't be certain.

Beer nuts on the bar top. The drinks came in their little

glasses crammed with ice, and Jack remembered why he liked the place, what he'd missed about America. Ice, and narrow straws you used to extract your drink as though you were a hummingbird.

They clinked glasses.

At the end of the bar a greasy-looking man drank a boiler-maker. "Lovebirds," he said. "How very revolting."

Jack put his hand on the bar and pivoted on his stool in order to give the man a serious look. "Hold on, there, Samuel Beckett," he said.

"Samuel who, now."

"Beckett," said Jack. "You look like him."

"*You* look like him," said the false Beckett from his bar stool. It was hard to tell whether he was Irish or drunk.

"How about that," said Sadie. "You do."

"I know," said Jack, irritated.

"You're wearing a scarf," she observed, and touched the fringe of it.

"It's cold."

"You're wearing a woman's scarf. It's got polka dots on it."

"Are polka dots only for women?" said Jack.

"I do not look like Samuel Beckett," said Samuel Beckett at the end of the bar. "I look like Harry Dean Stanton."

"Who?" Jack asked.

"The actor," Sadie explained. "You know." She tried to think of a single Harry Dean Stanton movie and failed.

"Unfamiliar."

"Another?" asked the bartendress, and Jack nodded. She put down the drinks and scooped up the money from the pile Jack had left on the bar.

"He's my cousin," said the man.

"Samuel Beckett?"

"Harry Dean *Stanton*," said Samuel Beckett.

"Sorry," said Jack. "I lost track."

"He's my cousin."

"Really?"

"No. But sometimes people buy me drinks because they think so."

"I'll buy you a drink," said Sadie, and she flagged the bartendress.

"Ah," said Samuel Beckett, "maybe it's *me* she loves."

"It is not," said Jack.

She *was* the sort of person who liked bar stools, after all. It felt easier to talk to somebody next to you than across, a slantwise intimacy in which you looked at the person less but could bump shoulders or elbows more. Even so she was astounded when his hand landed in her lap. It didn't feel carnal, but architectural: whatever they were building wouldn't work unless they put things down right the first time.

"You mind?" he asked.

His fingers were nowhere too personal. Just the outer part of her thigh. They were pleasant there. The bar balanced on the edge of the turnpike; she balanced inside of the bar.

Everything was a haze of smoke. Sadie lit a cigarette and offered one to Jack.

He shook his head. "Must protect the voice."

"Protect it for what?"

"The opera," said Jack.

"You sing opera?"

"I might one day. I'm thinking of going to clown college. I have aspirations."

"Clown aspirations? I hate clowns."

"Too late. You've met me, you like me, I'm a clown."

"Aspiring clown."

"I've clowned a bit. I'm more of a sad clown."

"I'm suing you," said Sadie. "For alienation of affection. *Clowns*."

"Everyone thinks they hate clowns. But they're not actual clowns they're thinking of."

"They're actual clowns *I'm* thinking of. A clown pinched me once. At a circus."

"Pinched."

"On the."

"On your arse," he said, laughing.

She laughed, too. "Arse, is it. What sort of man are you?"

"What a question."

"I mean, from where? Your accent's American, but you don't talk like an American."

"I am," he said, turning on his English accent, "of dual nationality. English and American. What do you call it? Aaaassss."

"Aaaassss," she agreed.

"Too many *A*s and too many *S*s."

"My mother would call it a bottom."

"Now that," said Jack, "I cannot condone."

"I do hate clowns," she said wickedly, loving the taste of wickedness in her mouth.

That was the thing about being in love: you were allowed to hate things. You didn't need them anymore. When the clown had pinched her, she'd wondered what it meant, whether the clown was attracted to her, whether she should engage him in conversation.

"Well, then," he said, "I'd better be a puppeteer. No, that's right, you hate puppets as well. What is it that you like?"

She thought about it. "Boats," she said.

"All right," he said. "I'm off to be a shipwright."

From the end of the bar Samuel Beckett called, "I have a favor to ask."

The bartendress said, "Keith, knock it off."

"Keith," said Samuel Beckett.

"Your name's Keith?" Sadie asked. She was already fishing in her pockets for some money to slip him.

"In this life, yes," said the man with exaggerated dignity. "Meredith I may ask them anything I like."

The bartendress said, "Half an hour and I'll walk you home."

"Meredith I must go home *now* and these fancy people will walk me."

"Keith—"

"It is not far away," said Samuel Beckett, or Keith—it was hard to think of him as Samuel Beckett now that he was definitively Keith, but they put their minds to it—"But I could use some assistance."

They looked at the bartendress.

"He's harmless," she said. "But he's afraid of the dark."

"With *reason* Meredith."

"With reason," agreed the bartendress.

"We'll walk you home," said Sadie.

"I guess we'll walk you home," said Jack.

They dismounted their bar stools. Jack could put his feet right to the ground. Sadie had to slide and drop. Samuel Beckett climbed down slowly and deliberately, chary of the pivot, as though his head were a tray of brimming glasses he was afraid of spilling, but then he didn't stop—his knees folded, and he went almost to the floor before Jack caught him by the elbow.

"You *are* wearing a ladies' scarf," the man told Jack. Up close he looked less like Samuel Beckett. For instance, he was wearing a jacket with little cloth button-down epaulets and a tag that said MEMBERS ONLY, and his eyes were too far apart, like a hammerhead shark's.

"That's all you got?" Jack said. "You'll catch your death."

"Not if it catches me first," said Samuel Beckett gloomily.

Sadie and Jack pulled on their winter coats, red down for her, black wool for him. Gloves, hats. Somehow it was agreed that they would walk arm in arm, Samuel Beckett in the middle, Jack and Sadie on either side.

"I live on Marlborough," he said. "You know where that is?"

"I do not."

"I do," said Sadie. "So were you mugged?"

The weight of Samuel Beckett pulled at them as they walked. They followed him as though he were a dray horse. The cold had turned bitter: they'd drunk right through the start of real winter.

"Careful," said Jack.

"You're a beautiful couple," said Samuel Beckett. Sadie was laughing as they slipped on the icy sidewalk. "I pronounce you man and wife. No I was never mugged. But sometimes in the snow I get too sad to keep on. So I sit. And then I put my head down. And one night I slept out all night and I woke up in jail."

"Heavens," said Jack.

"Too sad to keep on," said Sadie. "I get that."

"Do not, do not. My dear," he said. "Or we could. Shall we sit? Look, a curb. Look, another one. It's nothing but curbs this part of town." He began to go down and then gave Jack a dirty look. "Why are you pulling at my arm?"

"I'm keeping you afloat, man," said Jack, who by then was inexplicably smoking a cigarette.

"I thought you didn't smoke," said Sadie.

"Not much. Come, Sammy Becks. This way?"

"It's this way," said Sadie. "If we aren't sitting down. We could sit down."

"We aren't."

"Aren't we?" said Samuel Beckett. "Perhaps all my life what I wanted was a woman who'd sit on a curb with me."

They walked for what seemed like hours, turning corners and doubling back, through the numbered alleys and alphabetical streets of the Back Bay. With every step Sadie's feet rang in the cold like a slammed gate. "Where are we?" she asked and Samuel Beckett pointed and said, "Exeter."

It was possible, thought Jack, that they had walked to Exeter, where he'd worked in a theater box office and rented a room from a theatrical couple—not theatrical in the sense of *working in the theater* but in the sense of: she was twenty years older with a blond crew cut, smelled of burnt roses, and he wore a pince-nez and sewed all of their gaudy extraordinary clothing, pin-tucked and double-breasted and circus-striped. He'd loved both of them, was disquieted by their adoration of each other, an equation he could never quite solve.

But the Exeter in question was a cinema, the marquee said so; the cinema was named after the street. The doors opened, and costumed people walked into the night. A tall man with drawn-on eyebrows pulled a blue feather boa tight around his neck. A platform-shoed and corseted person in a sequined jacket and majorette shorts squared a top hat over ears; you could divine nothing of the person at the center of all the makeup and sequins except a sort of weary bliss. Around them, more people in sequins and tulle, lipstick and lamé. Their appearance struck Jack like the revelation at night of some kind of luminescent animal, jellyfish or firefly: a single instance would be uncanny, but the whole group made you accept the miracle and think of holy things.

"What is happening?" said Sadie.

"Midnight movie," said Samuel Beckett, turning into an alley.

"We've been down this alley," said Jack.

"There's a bar."

"Bars are closed."

"We can knock on the door. They'll let me in."

What had seemed like a lark and good deed now felt like a con to Sadie, but she couldn't figure out its next gambit. Let him sit on the curb after all. That might be safer. She said to Jack, "Maybe we should just take him back to Meredith."

"Bars are closed," Jack repeated. "Besides, if we don't get him home, we'll regret it forever."

Forever? she thought. They'd known each other six hours. She cuddled up a little closer to Samuel Beckett and tried to feel Jack through him. All right, she wouldn't go home, though she wanted to, her little studio apartment, too disordered for a visitor of any kind, particularly for one she wanted to—what verb was she looking for? *Impress*, she decided, followed by *fuck*.

The ice in the alley was glacial; she could feel its peaks and valleys through the soles of her shoes. At the end, Dartmouth Street again. She turned right. The men followed. They would go to Marlborough Street and find the man's house. "Almost there," she declared. Then the man said, in front of a small building with a heavy glass and oak door, "We've found it, we're home."

"I thought you said Marlborough Street," said Sadie.

"Near," he said. "*Near* Marlborough Street."

"Where are your keys?" asked Jack.

They held him up by the crooks of his elbows as he tried to find his pockets by chopping at himself all over with the sides of his hands. But then he lurched at the door and said, "Sometimes," and pushed the door open. "Thought so."

Late night, a marbled alcove, three steps up. The marble did its work, awed the people. They fell quiet.

After a moment the man said, in a wondering, deciding whisper, "Top floor."

He doesn't live here, Sadie thought. *We are trespassing.* She could not say so.

The elevator was old, with an iron accordion gate, and could fit only one person at a time, a rocket to the moon in a silent film.

"All right," whispered Jack to Sadie. "You put him in. I'll run up and call for the elevator. Then you come next."

Jack went up the stairs light-footed as he could. He thought he might love the strange young woman he'd met just outside a puppet, on the coast of a puppet, in the harbor of a puppet, and as always with women he was trying to decide how much to lie about and how much to be discon-certingly truthful about—he'd never hit the right cocktail in his twenty-seven years on earth—panting now, at first he'd been ahead of the elevator and he heard it gaining on him, a capsule full of drunkenness, so he took the stairs two at once—it felt impossible—and ended up with time enough to stand at the top and wait. Jack didn't want to see the man's apartment: he imagined a depressing disaster, vivid in his mind because he himself might end up in such a place, piles of magazines, empty glasses with the merest tint of drink left in, a veil of intoxication over everything. The lights in the hallway were on. Lights blazed in hallways around the clock in America. Forget the streets of gold. Here came Samuel Beckett, Samuel Beckett in a Members Only jacket. By the time he got there he seemed to have forgotten where he was going.

"Oh, good, it's you!" he said to Jack, full-voiced, catch-ing his finger in the accordion gate. "Son of a *bitch*."

Then Sadie ran up the stairs, too. The two men waited for her at the top, as though she were a bride at a wedding.

"Which door," she whispered. There were only two, one that said PH and the other with no marking at all. It wasn't too late to leave. They could deliver the man to the police department like a foundling infant.

"Keys?" Jack said to Samuel Beckett.

The man said, "Oh I never." He faced the unmarked door, either unlocking it with the power of his mind or trying to make the doorknob hold still in his drunken eyesight. Then he reached and turned it and the door swung open.

They stepped together into the hallway. In the dark, Jack inhaled, waiting for any one of the scents of sadness: human urine, animal urine, years of cigarette smoke, mildew, chronic and ashamed masturbation. But it smelled fine. Pleasant even, some old-fashioned pine cleaner at work.

Samuel Beckett—he wasn't actually Beckettian, just possessed of a triangular head, which was also true of Jack himself—found the light switch, and revealed a small, tidy, beautifully furnished apartment. Snug, with a green chesterfield sofa, a brown leather chair. Sadie felt more drunkenly certain that they were trespassing. She examined the man for evidence, then the apartment itself. Did they belong to each other? No photographs but art, muddy etchings down the hallway, abstract alabaster sculptures on the end tables. She needed a glass of water.

"What now?" said Jack, and Samuel Beckett said, "Bed."

"You need to go to the bog first," said Jack.

"The what?"

"The toilet."

"The restroom," said Samuel Beckett. "Winston Churchill's advice."

"Don't call me Winston Churchill," said Jack. "Of all the Englishmen I might be mistaken for!"

"His advice," said Samuel Beckett. "Never pass up the opportunity to use the loo."

"Ah. You need help?"

Samuel Beckett shook his head. "In this field I got nothing but experience."

The bathroom door closed and for a moment there was nothing to do. *Bar the door*, thought Jack. *We live here now.* But the girl looked nervous, and he understood it was his job to calm her.

"You're all bundled up," he said. He had taken off his black peacoat and hung it on a hook by the door. Now he came over and unzipped her down jacket, then thrust his left arm down her right sleeve so that both their arms lay along each other. He felt her wrist. She put her hand beneath his sweater, then beneath his T-shirt, and rested it on his bare boyish waist. They had not kissed. No matter what happened, this was a story, a good one. She was already working on how to tell it. Something thumped in the bathroom.

"Should we break down the door?" said Sadie.

"No!" shouted Samuel Beckett from the other side.

He emerged pantless, in his jacket with the epaulets, a white button-up-the-front shirt, blue-striped boxer shorts as baggy as bloomers. He seemed ready for bed in another century, future or past: hard to tell. "Ah, the newlyweds. I'm drunker," he explained. "I do believe I'm drunker. Scientific fact. Bed, I think."

"You need help?"

"Kind sir," he said to Jack.

The two men bumped down the narrow hallway. Just over the threshold Jack picked up a frame from a dresser top and said, "Is that—"

"Me," said the man.

"But with you," he said. "Is that—Dorothy Parker?"

"Dear Dorothy," the man agreed.

"Why are you dressed as—"

"Costume party. Railroad theme."

"Do you want your jacket off?"

"Why, where are we going?" But he shrugged it off. His shirt beneath also had epaulets.

"Epaulets all the way down," said Jack.

"Epaulette," he answered. "Nice girl. French."

Dear Dorothy! Thank God! thought Sadie, and realized she, too, needed the bog, the loo, the toilet. She went in. Everything was white except the toilet paper, which was pink, the scented kind, and the toilet seat was cushioned and it hissed beneath her, and between those details and an actual photo of himself with an actual famous person, she could relax. Who was he? Not important. The apartment was his. She was alone for the first time in hours, and she consulted her soul: *Yes, it was a good night.* The photograph explained everything. They had solved a problem together, and that was a good sign, a fine foundation for whatever came next. She scooped some water into her mouth from the tap and realized she was still cold. The lukewarm water was velvet in her mouth, the mirror too high for her to see anything other than her forehead. She went to join the men.

Had he made his bed, or had somebody made it for him, the white sheet folded with precision over a sky-blue blanket, white pillows that had been plumped and smoothed. Sadie herself had not made her own bed in years: it was one of the most liberating things about being a grown-up. Jack, though, was a maker of beds, a love letter you mailed to yourself in the morning that arrived at the end of the day. They never should have married, probably. They couldn't know all the ways their marriage would be mixed: she was punctual, he was late; she would never willingly drink a gin and tonic, she had a sweet tooth, he liked bitter greens and smoked haddock and oversalted his food. He didn't drive, and she didn't like to; he was (he would have denied it) gregarious, she was a misanthrope of the purest kind, one who didn't let on but cloaked her misanthropy with manners. He didn't mind a bit of thievery—restaurant salt and pepper shakers he took a fancy to, flowers from other people's gardens—while she was a rigid moralist about ill-gotten gains, returned every extra bit of money, corrected sales clerks who rang her up wrong. They were both cowards. She was an only child, he had three sisters. He liked horror movies, she liked dirty jokes, he was deep down a prude, they were both bad with money. All the dives where they drank in those days are gone, that's how old they are now.

Sadie pulled the covers back, and Jack helped their drunk into bed.

"Should we put him on his side?" she said. "So he doesn't choke."

"Choke on what," said Samuel Beckett.

Sadie waited a moment before she said, "Your own vomit."

He opened his eyes, which drunkenness and gravity had pulled so far apart they seemed in danger of sliding off opposite sides of his head. "I don't get sick."

"I think we better," she said to Jack.

"If not tonight then another," he answered, and even he did not know whether he meant *He'll choke another night* or *We'll sleep together another night.* "Heave-ho," he said to Samuel Beckett, who allowed himself to be turned.

They had delivered him home, they had saved him, they went to go. "Where's Dorothy Parker?" whispered Sadie. But the photo was nothing like she'd imagined, a giant group shot, and she said, "Where?" and Jack said, "There and there," but they were so far apart! and she wasn't convinced, honestly, that it was either one of them.

THE SOUVENIR MUSEUM

Perhaps she should have known that she would find her lost love—her Viking husband, gone these many years, on the island of Funen, in the village of his people. Asleep in the hut of the medicine woman, comforted by the medicine woman, loved by the medicine woman, who was (it turned out) a podiatrist from Aarhus named Flora. The village itself was an educational site and a vacation spot where, if you wanted, you could wear a costume and spin wool for fun. As for Aksel—was he Joanna's common-law ex-husband, or ex-common-law husband? Eleven years ago they had broken up after living together for ten. "Broken up": one summer Aksel had left for Denmark and she never heard from him again.

Not *never*. He sent an apologetic postcard from London. But never after that, nothing for eleven years. She'd married, been made a mother, lost a mother, been legally divorced, finally was fully orphaned by her father's death. Her father, who had been heartbroken when Aksel disappeared, for his own sake. Who else would breakfast with him on white wine and oysters? Who would discuss the complexities of savory pies, pork, kidney, the empanada versus the Cornish pasty? They had adored each other. Enormous and bearded, condescending and fond, ravenous, sad-eyed, the pair of them. Mortifying, when Joanna thought about it, how alike they were: her friends commented on it. It was her father who referred to Aksel as a common-law husband, when he was in every way a boyfriend, including the way she thought about him, years later: with a lechery untouched by having to legally untangle.

After the funeral, her father's cluttered bedroom was like the tank of an animal who perhaps had died or perhaps had fallen asleep behind the greenery: she looked and looked for him. Nothing felt definitive. The watch was in the nightstand drawer beneath an expired passport, heavy and silver, a steam locomotive on its case, a yellowing sticker on the back: PLEASE BRING TO AKSEL. She read and reread the sticker. Leo, her son, was like his grandfather drawn to long-ago things, though nine-year-old Leo particularly loved weapons and had nearly every morning for two years drawn in pencil an armory. He liked blades best: swords, bayonets, the occasional flail. He was not allowed toy weapons, though they came into the house the back way. That is, in Lego boxes: bow and arrows the size of safety pins, pistols that snapped into the tense and insatiable hands of Legomen.

She turned the watch over in her palm. Perhaps Leo could get interested in horology. She pictured him hunched over a watchmaker's bench and thought about tossing the note and keeping the watch. Instead, she transferred it from her father's nightstand into her own. *Bring*, he'd written. Not *mail*, not *get*. The sticker was as close to a will as he'd left, goddamn him. She should probably—she thought, aware of the daft expression already on her face—attempt to honor it.

It took a year to settle the estate, sell the condo, come into the little bit of money that would allow them for the first time to travel abroad. Joanna bought Leo the bunk beds that she had wanted as a child. When she went to wake him up for school in the morning, she never knew at what altitude she would find him. That morning he'd hidden himself in the top bunk among the stuffed animals and the alligator-patterned comforter cover, which had disgorged its comforter. Then she saw one bare heel. Even his heel was fast asleep and dear.

"Leo," she said.

The heel disappeared. He balled himself up under the covers as though winding himself awake. Then he sat up and blinked, bare-chested and skinny.

"What do you think about Vikings?" she asked him.

"They're not my favorite," he said, and put out his hand. "Glasses?"

He was newly bespectacled, having failed a vision test at school. Because he hadn't cared she'd picked him out a pair of square black glasses, so that he looked not like the bookish skinny wan pubescent boy he was, but a skinny wan 1980s rocker. *Wow*, he'd said, stepping out of the optician's, scanning the parking lot, the parking lot trees, the Starbucks and the Staples. *Wow*. Just like that, both he and the world looked different.

She found his glasses on a bookshelf and handed them up. "Vikings aren't your favorite?"

He scooted to the end of the bunk and climbed down the ladder. "I like Romans." The underpants he'd slept in were patterned with lobsters, too small. "Vikings didn't *really* have horns on their helmets. Did you know that?"

"I did not," she said.

For a year and a half, before Leo could read but after he'd begun to talk, Joanna had known everything in his head, thoughts and terrors, facts and passions. He'd belonged to Fairyland then; afterward, to books and facts. Now he had thoughts all the time that she hadn't put in his head, which she knew was the point of having children but destroyed her.

"So," she said. "I have a friend in Denmark. I was thinking we might go there this summer."

Leo sat at his desk and picked up a pencil. In the voice he used for lying, or when he cared too much about something, he said, "If we go, could we go to Legoland?"

"I thought that was in California."

"Real Legoland," Leo explained. "*Danish* Legoland. Denmark's where Lego was invented."

"You're not too old for all that?"

The glasses magnified his incredulous look. He looked like a 1950s TV journalist who knew he was being lied to. "Mommy, you *know* I like Lego."

"Yes," she said. "Of course." Lego: its salient angles, its minute ambitions. On her own childhood trips, Joanna had been at the mercy of her father's interests. He drove the car; he decided where to stop it. Not amusement parks, not tourist traps. Instead: war museums, broken-toothed cemeteries, the former houses of minor historic figures, with tables set for dinner—soup tureens and fluted spoons—and swords crossed over the fireplace. Joanna, aged nine, ten, forever, had wanted to go to Clyde Peeling's Reptiland. To the Mystery Spot, where ball bearings rolled uphill. To Six Flags Over Anywhere. A sign for Legoland would have driven her mad with longing, would have made her whine, even though whining—her mother would point out—had never gotten her anywhere. Her father would have driven on to some lesser Civil War battlefield to inspect an obelisk.

Leo was a child of divorce, and all his own vacations were airplane volleys from Rhode Island to California and back. The two of them had never really traveled together.

"All right," she said. "We'll go to Legoland."

She had already renewed their passports, bought the tickets, reserved a Volvo with a GPS. But you had to give a child the illusion of choice.

Legoland was overwhelmingly yellow, and Leo, abashed, hated it. The rides had electric signs outside which estimated how long you'd have to stand in line to ride them. The log flume was a forty-five-minute wait. The polar roller coaster, an hour and five. It was an ordinary overcrowded amusement park. They had flown from Boston to Paris, then Paris to Billund, to end up at *this* place, the first day of their vacation. He wondered how long they would have to stay for his mother to get her money's worth. She could be grim about expensive fun. The crowds of children upset him, blonder than the blondest American blond. *Flaxen hair*, he thought.

Like from a book. Flaxen hair and cornflower-blue eyes, though he'd never seen flax or cornflowers in real life. If he had, he might think, *Blue as a Danish child's eyes, pale as a Danish child's mullet*. The blondness itself seemed evil to Leo. A blond child who screeches and steps on your foot is compelled by its blondness; a blond mother who hits you with her stroller—here comes another one, rushing after her child, who is attempting to climb into the lap of the life-sized Lego statue of Hans Christian Andersen—does it out of pure towheadedness.

In America he would have cried out, but in Legoland he felt he had to bear it.

Even the gift shop was disappointing. He'd been imagining something he couldn't imagine, some immense box that would allow him to build—what? A suit of Lego. A turreted city big enough to live in. Denmark itself. He did not dream in Lego, not anymore, but sometimes he still raked his hand through the bins of it beneath his bed as a kind of rosary, to remind himself that the world, like Lego, was solid and mutable, both.

Joanna, too, found Legoland terrible; Joanna, too, could not confess. It was a kind of comfort, because Aksel had always been exhausting on the subject of Denmark versus America. Denmark was beautiful, and so were Danes; America was crass, and every moment of American life was a commercial for a slightly different form of American life, you could not so much as enjoy a hamburger without having your next hamburger advertised to you, though the hamburgers would be exactly the same: spongy and flavorless. "Americans have garbage taste," he would say, tucking into an American banana split. "Not you, Johanna." He always added a spurious *h* to her name. "But someday you will go to Denmark, and taste the ice cream, and you will understand." Clearly the man had never been to Legoland, where even ice cream required a half hour's wait in line, and then was a tragedy of dullness.

They stopped at a self-serve slush stand that allowed you to mix all the flavors you wanted into a tall plastic glass that looked like a bong. Leo's personal cocktail came out army green. This had always happened to his Play-Doh, too, when it got mixed together. He drank it with his eyes closed and winced. He most resembled his late grandfather when unhappy.

"Poor bunny, you're jet-lagged. Here. Let's sit." They sat on the bench next to the Lego Hans Christian Andersen, and Joanna had a sense that they shouldn't, they should leave the space clear for people who wanted pictures of themselves with a Lego Hans Christian Andersen. But why should those people get their way?

"I'm not jet-lagged," he said.

"Do you want to just go to the hotel room?"

"Is the hotel room in Legoland?"

"Yes," she said.

"Oh." Then, "I hate it here."

"Denmark?"

He looked at her aghast. "This isn't *Denmark*," he said. "Can we go? It's not what I thought it would be like."

"Yes," said Joanna, grateful and motherly, a *good* mother, indulgent. "What did you think it would be like?"

But she knew. In our private Legolands we are the only human people.

"I'll tell you what," she said, and she handed Leo her phone. "You choose. Wherever you want to go, we'll go. I know Vikings aren't your favorite, but I have a friend at that Viking village—"

"What Viking village?"

"*A* Viking village," she said. "We'll go at the end of the week. In the meantime, do some research. Plan the next three days. If you want, we can come back to Legoland—"

"I'm never going to come back to Legoland," he said passionately.

When our children love what we love, it is a blessing, but O when they hate what we hate!

Denmark was studded with little museums dedicated to misery and wealth and the unpleasant habits of men, and Leo wanted to go to every one. He was warming to the Vikings. There was a kind of gentle boredom to Denmark, which was in itself interesting: archaeological museums whose captions were entirely in Danish, with displays of pottery, shards and nails and swords and bits of armor. To become interested in a boring subject was a feat of strength. A splinter of Viking armor was more interesting than the whole suit, to Leo, because even though it was in a glass box it might fit in your pocket. Perhaps he liked bits because of his nearsightedness—now that he had glasses, it was disquieting what loomed on the horizon—but entire objects told the entire story, and therefore belonged to everyone. Looking at a piece of a thing, he might think, deduce, discover something nobody ever had, which was all he wanted in the world.

They took a ferry to the island of Ærø. In the old ship-yard Leo made rope with a crank-operated machine, and, with the help of a blacksmith, a plain iron hook. The black-smith was a lean man with a sad, rectilinear face and hair the color of clapboard. The black iron glowed orange when you put it in the forge, and when you hammered it orange sparks flew off and then you were left with something so black and solid you couldn't imagine it had ever been otherwise.

They went to the Workhouse Museum, three maritime museums, the Danish Railway Museum. Of course Joanna missed her father, seeing his dullest passions alive in his grandson. Who else could love trains so much that they were still interesting in a museum, where they were robbed of their one power, movement? Not Joanna, but she could love somebody who did. She felt a useless pride in Leo's peculiar enthusiasms; Leo's pleasant father liked action movies and video games, like any American boy.

Joanna had arrived with three pieces of Danish: *Taler du engelsk?* (The answer was always *yes, I do*), *tak!*, and the words for *excuse me*, which she remembered because it sounded—she thought it sounded; she had a terrible ear—like *unskilled*. *Unskilled! Taler du engelsk? Tak!* Soon she picked up the vocabulary of ice cream—Aksel was right, vanilla ice cream in Denmark was hallucinogenically delicious—*kugler, waffler, softice, flødebolle*, though a month after they got home Joanna would wake up in the middle of the night wondering, *Is the Danish word for thanks pronounced* tock *or* tack? And which pronunciation had she used? The wrong one, she was sure.

Aksel's watch was in her pocket. She'd put it in a Ziploc

bag to keep it clean and hadn't so much as wound it. It wasn't hers to wind. She liked the weight of it about her person.

Did she still love Aksel? No, but the memory of him came in handy sometimes.

They found the Souvenir Museum the old-fashioned way: first one roadside sign, then another. The museum was in the grounds of a modest castle. Like Legoland, the name was full of promise. Souvenir: a memory you could buy. A memory you could *plan* to keep instead of being left with the rubble of what happened.

A teenage girl with a drowsy, dowsing head slid a pamphlet across the ticket desk, and then pointed to the door to the museum. Leo opened the pamphlet. The museum was made of six rooms. He was startled to see that the last one was called Forbidden Souvenirs.

A year ago Leo might have asked his mother what *Forbidden Souvenirs* meant. Now he was seized with a terrible, private fear that he didn't want her to disturb or dispel. He read books about war; his mother didn't. Soldiers took souvenirs: ears, teeth, shrunken heads, scalps.

His mother, innocent, admired the first glass case, which was filled with salt and pepper shakers. Two Scottish terriers, black and white. One Scottish terrier (salt) lifting its leg in front of a red fire hydrant (pepper). The next glass case was also filled with salt and pepper shakers. There was a density to the collection that felt like a headache, or the physical manifestation of dementia, where the simplest items had to be labeled for meaning: china Eiffel Towers marked PARIS, cheap metal London Bridges marked LONDON. It had clearly been somebody's private collection, a problematic Dane's hoard. Surely all the salt and pepper shakers had been made in one vast factory in Japan or China, then stamped with geographic locations and shipped off.

"After this," she said, "we'll go to the Viking village. Your grandfather would have hated this place. What's the matter?"

I don't want to see, he thought, but also he did.

He was stepping into Forbidden Souvenirs. It took him a moment to figure out what he was looking at: coral, ivory, alligator shoes, exotic game of all sorts, pillaged antiquities.

"Are you all right?"

"Yes," he said.

A faceless mannequin wore a leopard jacket over nothing, its skinny white featureless body obscene. "Grandma had a mink stole," Joanna said. "I can't remember what we did with it."

Some of the objects flaunted the original animal: the head of an alligator biting shut a pocketbook, the dangling back paws of a white fox on a stole. Was that better or worse than the elephant carved out of an elephant tusk, the tortoise incised into the tortoise shell?

"I thought there would be ears," said Leo. "From the enemy."

"What enemy?"

"I don't know," said Leo helplessly. "The enemy dead."

"No ears," said Joanna in an improbably cheery voice. She gestured at the glass case. "Nothing to worry about."

"I wasn't," he said. But he had been, the worry was in him, the fear of seeing something he shouldn't have, human, severed. The feeling was traumatic and precious.

"Anyhow," she said.

"Do they pretend there?" he asked.

"Do they what where?"

"Pretend at the Viking village. Dress up and say they're Vikings."

"Oh. Not sure. Why?"

"The Renaissance Faire," he said darkly.

They'd gone to a Ren Faire when Leo was four. He'd gotten lost in an iron maze built of child-sized cages and began to sob—she had a picture of him that she'd taken before she'd noticed the tears—and a man dressed as an executioner had to talk him out, gesturing with his plastic ax. Leo liked to bring it up from time to time, evidence of Joanna's bad judgment. He liked history. He did not like grown-ups in fancy dress.

She said, "It'll be great."

"That's what you said about Legoland."

Had she? "Leo—"

"I *said* I didn't want to go."

"No, you—"

"Yes I did," he said. The words were underlined, she heard it, and later she would understand it as the first sign of adolescence, and she would forgive him, but she didn't forgive him now.

"Well," she said, "we're going."

The eyes of a half dozen taxidermy animals were upon them, as though betting on who'd win the argument, and who'd end up in the museum. Then the humans turned and wordlessly went from the room.

In the morning they drove to Odin's Odense, their bags packed in the trunk of the rented car. That night they would go on to Copenhagen, then fly back to the States. Joanna looked in the rearview mirror at sulking Leo. Next year he would be tall enough to ride up front, but for now he was in the back seat. *You get to choose*, she'd said, and she'd hoped to finagle him into believing that a trip to the Viking village had been his choice. What she'd endured for him! Three days of stultifying museums. They had traveled together beautifully, sleeping in the same room for the first time since his infancy. Ruined now. She knew the ruination she felt was her own treacherous heart.

The car's built-in GPS brought them deeper into the suburbs, red-tiled roofs, no businesses. "This doesn't look right," said Leo from the back, hopefully. But the GPS knew what it was doing, and there they were. Odin's Odense.

They had to pass through a little un-Viking modern building that housed admissions, a gift shop, and flush toilets. Joanna wondered whether she should ask after Aksel, but what if he had a Viking name? The old woman behind the counter thrust a map at her and frowned encouragingly. The museums of the world are filled with old women, angry that nobody will listen to them, their knowledge, their advice. Joanna hadn't told Leo why they were here, in case it came to nothing.

She gave him the map. "Here. It's in English."

He consulted it and said casually, "There's a sacrificial bog."

"That might come in handy."

They walked together into the Viking village on one of those days of bright sunshine, the sky so blue, the clouds so snowy white, everything looked fake. Though why was that? Why, when nature is its loveliest, do human beings think it looks most like the work of human beings?

Was her detection system still tuned to Aksel's frequency? Once she could walk into any room and know he was there. She detected nothing.

The Viking huts were 89 percent thatched roof, like gnomes in oversized caps. A teenage boy in a tunic and laced boots ducked out of one, his arms laden with logs. He gave Joanna a dirty look, and she understood that he was mad at his mother, wherever she was, in whatever century, and therefore mad at all mothers.

Leo, too. He pointed to a small structure with no roof and said gloomily, "I think this is the old smithy."

There was nothing smithish about the old smithy. Joanna put her hands on her hips as though she were interested in smithery, though all she could feel was her heart beating warrantless through her body. She knew she and Leo would forgive each other. She knew that it was her duty to solicit forgiveness from everyone, but just then she was tired of men whose feelings were bigger than hers. She felt as though she'd grown up in a cauldron of those feelings and had never gotten out.

"Okay. What's next?"

"The medicine woman's hut."

Inside the medicine woman's hut, a squinty, hardy-looking woman of about sixty sat on a low bench, stirring an open fire with a stick.

"Hi, hi," said the woman. This was the jaunty way some Danish people said hello, and Joanna always felt exhilarated and frightened saying it back, as though she might pass for Danish a few seconds more. Which was worse, being found out as American, or as a fraud? It was a big space, illuminated by the fire and the sunlight coming through the front and back doors. The fire was directly underneath the highest part of the thatched ceiling: Viking fire safety. "Say hello," said Joanna to Leo.

A preposterous command. He didn't.

The medicine woman gestured to a low long bench across from her. In English, in the voice of the iron age, the woman said, "Welcome. Where do you stay?"

Were they supposed to be ancient, too?

Leo tried to feel it. Before Denmark, he hadn't realized how much he wished to be ancient. To be Danish. To be, he thought now, otherwise for a reason.

His mother said, "Last night, near Svendborg."

The medicine woman nodded, as though approving of this wisdom. "It is beautiful there." She withdrew her stick, inspected the end, stuck it back in. "You have been to Langeland? The 'big island,' you would call it?"

"No."

She nodded again. "You must."

She was the medicine woman: everything she said had the feel of a cure and a curse. Yes: they would go to the big island. It was inevitable.

On the big island, thought Joanna, she might forget her big mistakes; on the big island, they would scatter their memories, if not her father's ashes. They had not brought his ashes. There were too many of them.

"There is an excellent cold war museum," the medicine woman said.

What was a cold war, in the land of the Vikings?

"It has a submarine," the medicine woman said to Leo. "It is the largest in Europe, I believe. I took my son. Also minigolf close by. A good place to holiday, if you do not come here. Wouldn't you like to come to holiday here someday? That is what we do. We put on the clothes and—puh!—we are Vikings."

"Yes!" Leo said. "You mean, you stay here? You *sleep* here?"

"Of course!" She turned to the corner of the hut and said a sentence or two to a pile of blankets. Perhaps it was an ancient incantation. Nothing happened. She said it again. They could not find a single English cognate among the syllables.

The pile of blankets shifted. An animal? No. The blankets assembled themselves into a shadow of a man.

The shadow became an actual man, sitting up.

The actual man was Aksel.

He was eleven years older and much thinner and he had shaved his beard, even though he was now a Viking. He'd always had long, squintish eyes; they had acquired luggage. He yawned like a bear, working all the muscles of his jaw; that is, he yawned like Joanna's long-ago love, the foreigner she'd fallen for when they had worked together on a college production of *True West*. Joanna had been prop mistress, and had collected twenty-seven working toasters from yard sales and Goodwills. Aksel directed, and had broken every one of those toasters in a single impassioned speech to the actors, sweeping them off a table while declaring, "I don't want you to act, I want you to react, I want you to *get mad*."

The medicine woman said, "Aksel's mother told us you were coming here with the boy."

Joanna nodded. She still didn't know what millennium they were supposed to be in. "You get mail here?"

"She texted." The medicine woman mimed with her thumbs.

"Johanna," said Aksel. That needless, endearing *h*.

How many time frames was she in? College, mid-twenties, the Iron Age, the turn of the last century. He was recognizable to her—she'd worried he wouldn't be—and beloved to her, too.

"What are you doing here?" he asked, in a serious voice.

It was a good question. He didn't look like her father. That might have been what brought her here. The watch could be mailed; Legolands were legion; but where in the world was a man like the man she'd just lost?

Her actual heart found the door behind which her metaphorical heart hid; heart dragged heart from its bed and pummeled it. Years ago she'd wondered what, exactly, constituted love: the state of emergency she felt all ten years of their life together? Not that the building was on fire; not that the ship was about to sink; not that the hurricane was just off shore, pulling at the palm trees: the knowledge that, should the worst happen, she had no plan of escape, not a single safety measure, she was flammable, sinkable, rickety, liable to be scrubbed from the map. That feeling was love, she'd thought then, and she thought it now, too.

"My father died," she said.

"Ah, Walter," said Aksel, and he rubbed his jaw dolefully. "I am sorry. Recently?"

"A year ago. I have something for you. We decided—this is Leo—we decided it was a good time to come to Denmark, to deliver it."

"Hello, Leo," said Aksel, who looked half in dreamland, populated as it was by Ancient Danes, long-ago girlfriends, and preteen American boys. "I am very glad to meet you."

"You know my *mom*?" said Leo.

"That friend I mentioned." Then to Aksel: "I Facebooked your mom, but I guess you're off the grid."

"I am very much upon," he said. "You just don't know my coordinates." He looked again at Leo and nudged the medicine woman's back with his knee. "This is Johanna," he said of Joanna. "This is Flora," he said of the medicine woman. "Shall we go for a walk, Johanna? Just for a moment."

The medicine woman turned to Leo. "Do you want to play a game? My son is doing so. Come, he will teach you." She got up and ushered Leo through the front door, and Joanna and Aksel went out the back, the fire smoking, a hazard, but the Vikings must have known what they were doing.

"I've thought of you often, Johanna," said Aksel. In the sunlight he was shaggy, his color was not so good, but he was beautiful, a beauty. His clothes smelled of smoke. He seemed a victim of more than recreational Vikinghood.

"You're on vacation," she said. "I thought perhaps you'd become a professional Viking."

"Ah, no. I am a software developer. Flora, she is a foot doctor. And you?"

"Bookkeeper."

He nodded. "You were always a keeper of books. Let us discuss what you have brought me."

The minute she pulled the watch from her purse she missed its weight. She opened the Ziploc bag, suddenly worried that watches were supposed to breathe.

"Ah!" said Aksel, mildly. He took the watch and put it instantly inside a pouch he had tied to his belt, as though any sign of modernity were shameful. "Walter knew I admired this watch. That is what you came to give me?"

"It's what my father wanted you to have."

"And only this."

He started walking, and she followed, her long-ago husband, her lost love, to the banks of the sacrificial bog, if bogs had banks. Aksel said, "But not the boy."

"Not the boy what?"

"He isn't my son."

"What? No! He's *ten*."

"Ah!" said Aksel. "My mother said you were coming with a boy, and Flora thought maybe. She has a keen sense for these things."

She saw on his face an old emotion, disappointment shading into woe. "What did *you* think?"

He turned to the bog. "I might have liked it. Flora has a son. It might have saved me."

"Saved you? Viking you, or *you* you?"

The bog said nothing. Aksel said, "I can love anyone," and took her hand. It was the first time he had touched her. A moment ago she'd thought that would be the last step of the spell, the magic word, the wave of the wand. But it wasn't.

I could lie, she thought. She'd never really lied, not like that, a lie you would have to see through, a first step on the road to a hoax, an entirely different life, where facts and dates and numbers were fudged. Leo *did* exist because of Aksel. He would not otherwise.

But then Aksel dropped her hand, as though he'd been joking. "Women are lucky. God puts an end to their foolishness. But men, we are bedeviled till the end of our days."

She said, with as much love as she could muster, quite a lot, "Fuck off."

"All right, Johanna."

"Why did you leave?"

"I didn't want—" But there he stopped. The Viking village was all around them, smoke in the air, the bleating of sheep who didn't know what millennium they were in, either. Or perhaps they were goats. She couldn't always tell the difference.

"What didn't you want?" she asked him.

He shook his head. "A fuss."

"Jesus. I want the watch back."

"We might have married," he said. "But then it seemed as though we should have done it at the start."

"Give me the watch. I'll sacrifice it to the bog."

"It's worth rather a lot."

"Then Leo should have it. My son. I mean, we spent four hours at the railway museum. I don't know what I was thinking, giving it to you."

He retrieved the watch from his pouch, his Viking pocketbook, and weighed it in his hand as though he himself would throw it bogward. Instead he wound it up—later, when Leo *did* become interested in old watches, she would discover this was the worst thing you could do, wind a dormant watch—and displayed it. First he popped open the front to exhibit the handsome porcelain face, the elegant black numbers. "Works," he remarked. Then he turned it over and opened the back.

There, in his palm, a tiny animated scene, a man in a powdered wig, a woman in a milkmaid's costume, her legs open, his pants down, his tiny pink enamel penis with its red tip tick-tock-ticking at her crotch, also pink and white and red. It was ridiculous what passed for arousing in the old days. She was aroused.

"Old Walter," said Aksel. "He lasted awhile, then. He started taking care of himself?"

"No. He got worse and worse. He was eighty."

"He never wanted to be," said Aksel in a sympathetic voice.

"I know it."

He offered the watch. "In four years, perhaps your boy will be interested."

Ah, no: it was ruined. Not because of the ticking genitalia, but because it was somebody else's private joke, and she the cartoon wife wanting in, in a robe and curlers and brandishing a rolling pin. Even a cartoon wife might love her rascal husband. She did.

"He wanted you to have it for a reason," she said.

Flora's son and Leo played a Viking game that involved rolling iron hoops down a hill. Flora's son was sullen and handsome, with green eyes and licorice breath, terrible at mime, and so he put his hands on Leo's to show how to hold the hoop and send it off, then looked Leo in the eyes to see if he'd gotten it, all with a kind of stymied intimacy that Leo understood as a precursor to grown-up love.

I will learn Danish, thought Leo. *I will never learn Danish.*

He turned to let the hoop go, and there was his mother, striding up the hill. Bowl her over for ten more minutes with this boy, ten more minutes in the Iron Age—where they had no concept of minutes—ten more minutes of this boy scratching his nose with the back of his wrist then touching the back of Leo's wrist with his Viking fingers. Bowl her down and stay.

No, of course not. The stride told him that they were leaving.

Would he have wished her away? Only if he could wish her back later.

And would she, Joanna, have wished her beloved Leo away? Only if she could also wish away his memory. To long for him forever would be terrible.

"See you later," said the Viking boy, who spoke English all along, and ran to gather the hoops.

NOTHING, DARLING,
ONLY DARLING, DARLING

"Who died and made you boss," Sadie asked Jack, and he answered, "Nobody. Everybody. How do you make somebody boss when you're dead, anyhow?"

Not *everybody* was dead, just a handful of significant people. Sadie's parents, Jack's sister, most recently Jack's nephew, blond Thomas of the passions, who'd gone to study piano in Poland and had stepped off a building at ten thirty in the morning. He'd been twenty-seven.

It was Thomas's death that convinced Sadie that she and Jack should finally marry. Without marriage, what was Thomas to her? She'd known him since childhood, a wiggling, insinuating, wonderful boy, a puppy, a darling; she'd known and loved him in every incarnation since. As a small child he liked to be tickled; as a teenager he'd hated haircuts and had worn his daffodil hair like a veil he intended to never lift; as a young man he developed a love of organized runs in which you had to crawl through mud and allow yourself to be shocked with live wires. It was not so much to know about a person, though enough to recognize a taste for obliteration. But without marriage he was, at his death, Jack's nephew, not hers. So they would marry at last, and Jack would arrange everything, because Sadie, while not a reluctant wife, was at thirty-nine a very reluctant bride.

Twenty years, or nearly. She had grown stout and he furious, but to be fair they'd tended in those directions all their lives. She would have been happy to marry at city hall, but Jack's parents, Michael and Irene Valert, astonishingly alive in their grief in Sussex, had suggested they marry in the church at the end of their drive. "Does your family have money?" Sadie had asked the first time she'd seen the former rectory his parents lived in. "Used to," Jack answered. But this was more than residual money. In America if you *used* to have money you probably had a relative or a former accountant in jail, and you lived in a two-bedroom apartment miles from the city of your dreams. The Valerts' house was the sort of place you'd rent in America for a single day in order to have that vulgar thing, a storybook wedding, to prepare yourself for the reality of married life.

Why not? Sadie had no relatives left to horrify with a church wedding. The Valerts had lost a child and lost a grandchild, and this was something that could be given. She thought of the wedding as a practical thing—she didn't even plan to invite friends to come over from the States—not knowing how Jack would take to it, the sentimental asshole, how much he wanted an English wedding himself. His parents had lived seventeen years in America, during which time they'd had him, their last child, and had developed a hatred of the country. Not *developed*, it wasn't brand-new, but now their hatred was expert. They'd repatriated when Jack went to college, and seemed like zoo animals stymied by the offspring they'd had in captivity.

She always forgot how some aspects of England were so *English*, so very *Masterpiece Theatre*: in order to get married in the village church, Sadie had to live with the elder Valerts for three weeks so that she might be registered as a spinster of the parish. Then the banns would be read, whatever that meant. Jack, on the other hand, could be where he pleased. What pleased him—"I *have* to," he said apologetically—was to go to Coventry, to an academic conference on puppetry in medieval mystery plays. So for the first week of Sadie's parish spinsterhood, she slept alone on one of the twin beds of the Valerts' guest room and was woken every day at three thirty a.m., which was, perversely, when dawn broke in Sussex in July. It wasn't the light that woke her, but the birds who saw the light and began laughing. Screeching. Saying in avian syllables designed to lacerate the eardrum, *Well, you wanted to get married!*

By the time Jack got back, his father was not speaking to Sadie for obscure reasons. Or not obscure: she didn't plan to change her name, or to wear a white dress, or to promise (as the outdated copy of the *Book of Common Prayer* he gave her suggested) to be "sober, quiet, and obedient."

"I might manage two of those at a time," she said. "But never all simultaneously." He didn't think that was funny. She hadn't known what a wedding meant in England: hats and child attendants and a dinner party to celebrate her engagement in which the women had to actually leave the dining room before the port was passed. No doubt they had all voted for Brexit. "You don't have to obey," said Michael Valert, "but I hope you'll consider children. I hope you're not so liberated as all that." Then, with a depth of feeling that startled her, he said, "I think we could all use something to look forward to."

They were joined in the church by a young rector with the booming voice of an old prophet, or actor, or train conductor, or possibly rector—Sadie had no experience with rectors. She knelt before him and thought of how much her little Yiddishe mama would have hated to see her do it. Then she stood up and they were married.

A month later they were in Holland, in Amsterdam: Jack and Sadie, honeymooners, newlyweds, middle-aged. Jack's phone said aloud, in its sexy English accent, "Prepare to turn right."

"But are you?" Sadie asked. "Prepared."

"Never."

"I didn't think so." She hooked her arm in his. With his other arm he pulled along their thunking suitcase.

They were staying in a houseboat across from the Anne Frank House.

"Does it move?" she asked.

"Does it *move*?" He'd always had a way of repeating her questions back, sometimes with love and sometimes with contempt and sometimes with wonder at the question itself. That was the case now. "No, I don't—it must be moored."

"Prepare to turn right," said the phone. Then, "Turn right."

Canal after canal, bakery after souvenir shop. You couldn't deny it: Holland was Dutch. "Looks good," said Jack, examining a menu outside a café, "we should come back," but Sadie was looking at the canal in front of them.

"I like a canal," she said.

"You hated Venice."

"Yes. True. Let Venice sink! Are we almost there?"

"Nearly. Prinsengracht. That's our address."

Houseboats all along the canal. Jack had asked his Dutch brother-in-law, Piet, for advice on where to stay, but Piet was from Rotterdam, had gone back there after his wife's death, insisted that Amsterdam was a Mickey Mouse city. "Come to Rotterdam," Piet said, and they would, after Amsterdam.

There it was: a white houseboat. It looked good, but you never really knew till you got in. Jack texted the landlady, and they went to a nearby bar to wait for her. When you fly overnight to Europe you're allowed to have beer for breakfast. That was one of their inviolable rules.

Beer for breakfast was what they had instead of children; trips to Europe every three years, indulgence. In nearly twenty years they had lived through the varieties of international practicalities: traveler's checks, phone cards, internet cafés—how devoted they'd been to internet cafés!—paying for wireless in coffee shops, cheap burner phones they needed to top up in shady convenience stores, and now: nothing. Their cell phone company offered unlimited data. They had filled their wallets with euros from an ATM at the airport and had credit cards with no international transaction fee. They would never be lost. They still could be cheated.

Occasionally Sadie thought about the life they might

have had with children. No better, probably. She was nearly forty. A child was unlikely but, yes, you elderly Valerts, technically possible, though none of your business. Jack was forty-six, his possibilities undimmed, except for the ones that involved fame and fortune. They'd chosen Amsterdam so that they could see Piet afterward, and because it was a city they had no memories of. They lived in America and wished they lived elsewhere. They'd always thought they might someday. Now *elsewhere*, geopolitically speaking, was narrowing to England, which was, according to Jack, as bad as where they were. Surely not, said Sadie. "I wish it weren't," said Jack.

Another reason to be legally married: the despots of the world still cared about things like that. They might need proof that they belonged together.

The landlady was a tall woman in her fifties, in a black crocheted cap shaped like a riding helmet. "Welcome!" she said as they crossed the street to the quay, pausing for a woman in a business suit on a bicycle, a dreadlocked white man on a bicycle, the handsomest old man Sadie had ever seen on a bicycle. "I am Cari. Your first time in Holland?"

"Yes," said Sadie.

"Yes," said Jack. "Well, I was here as a kid."

"Goot!" said Cari. "The lock!" She brandished a key on a small block of wood, and with her other hand cupped the padlock on the boat's hatch, fit them together, looked at first Jack and then Sadie to see if they understood this mystery: key, lock, access. They nodded.

She pulled up the hatch to reveal a small ladder down and announced, "You must always go backward," while descending forward. "Two hands. Here we go."

The inside of the boat was beautiful, painted in thick white blurring paint. The couches were white, the floor, the cabinets. The room was bigger than their living room at home, though low-ceilinged, with a line of square windows on both sides. The decorative pillows were pony patterned. Cari began to open cupboards—"You have a dishwasher, refrigerator. At night you put the padlock on the inside of the hatch, when you leave, on the outside. Garbage you deliver to the bridge—well, at any rate it is all here." She patted a binder.

"It's lovely," said Jack.

"Yes, it is," said Cari. She looked around the room. "It is very lovely."

She shook their hands, and then went up the ladder and out the hatch. "Shall I close?" she called down. "You have the lock!"

"Yes, please," said Jack.

The rules: Beer for breakfast. Don't carry your passports on you. Unpack as soon as you can. Sadie sat down on the sofa.

"Don't fall asleep!" Jack said.

"I won't."

The bed was beneath the wheelhouse, king-sized, on a shelf. Jack reckoned he would only just be able to sit up in bed, though Sadie would have no problem. Another rule: in any bed in any part of the world, they took their habitual sides, no matter how splendid or miserable. In this case, Sadie would face the water, and he the stone wall. That was all right. He took the little ladder to the right of the bed up to the old wheelhouse, now a sitting area with benches and a tiny bar and a framed picture of Anne Frank. Windows all around. To his right people walked along the quay and dodged cyclists; ahead, a huge church; to the left, the Anne Frank House, or the buildings all around the Anne Frank House, the front building that had always hidden it, the modern addition for admissions, with its gift shop and café.

Life was rotten, he thought, but happily, because Amsterdam was excellent, cold, the sky blue, his wife by law beer-sleepy in a boat, he in a glass box, ready to be admired. *Look at that man! He has rented a boat for his wife!*

You might change your life at any moment; they had. They could continue to. Before they'd met, Sadie was unpassported, untraveled: Europe, Jack thought (grandly, accurately), was a present he'd given her. To move is to change. Even if they had a child—this was his secret, that he'd begun to dream of children—they could tuck a kid under one arm and keep going. What could ever stop them from traveling, in this wide world? Plenty, it turned out: themselves, the world, the people in charge. Downstairs Sadie had already taken off her shoes and was reading a book on the elegant sectional sofa.

"How is it?" he asked.

"Not sure."

"What's it about?"

"Not sure about that, either." She put it aside. "Nice boat. Deluxe. Good job."

"It is nice, isn't it? Wait till you see the wheelhouse. Well done, me," he said to himself.

"Well done, *you*," she answered.

He began to unpack the suitcase, putting his shirts in one little cupboard and Sadie's dresses in another. He stepped into the bathroom to set out the cosmetic case—"Heated floors!" he said delightedly, unsure whether that was something one should take delight in—and returned to her on the sofa.

"Here," he said.

"You packed my slippers!" They were gray boots lined with artificial fur of a nearly malign softness. He knelt at her feet and put them on her with pantomime uxoriousness.

"I thought you might be happy to have them," he said. "I like your hair."

"Thank you."

"What color would you call that?"

"Amethyst," she said. She'd had it done once they were married, once nobody could disapprove. "That's what the girl called it. I thought I was too old."

"You're *not*," he said severely. "Maybe I'll dye my hair amethyst. Carnelian. Agate."

That was a joke. His hair was the sort of thick silvery gray that made people say, of men, *He's aged well*. He said again, "You're not too old."

"And yet here I am in my bedroom slippers." She closed her eyes in pleasure. "You've been here before?"

"When I was a teenager."

"Oh. You didn't say."

"My father accidentally walked us through the red-light district. It was a traumatic experience. We should probably go out," he said. "So we don't fall asleep."

"But it's so *nice* on our boat," said Sadie, stretching like the house cat she was. "How's the bed?"

"The bed is also nice."

"It's our honeymoon," she said. "Let's go to bed."

They woke up—an hour later? Three?—to daylight out the window by Sadie's head. *Porthole*, thought Sadie. But square: Did portholes have to be round? Her feet were hot. She was wearing her slippers but nothing else. She felt—*glad*. She wasn't sure gladness was an emotion she was familiar with. Happiness and joy, yes, durable, recognizable; gladness was thinner than that, historical, but useful. A shim to even out a wobbly sad table. She was glad they were in Amsterdam. She was glad that they had married.

"That's the Anne Frank Hoos," said Jack, pointing across her body.

"Hoos?"

"Hu-ees. I don't speak Dutch."

"You certainly don't."

"We should go out in the world," he said, and kissed her shoulder.

He wore a green shirt that she had ordered for him off the internet, intended for a Norwegian cheesemonger, and a pair of corduroys of a color he'd favored since he was three, brownish red. She had bought her flowered Swedish dress in New York City.

"Quite picturesque for a bridge where you leave garbage," he said as they stopped at its peak. They looked down at the moored barges on the margins of the canal and the tourist barges gliding down the middle.

"Where are the pot dealers?" said Sadie. "Where are the sex workers?"

"In the red-light district."

"Poor kid," she said, a cheek on his bicep; he was so much taller than she was, "were you scarred for life?"

"You tell me, Doctor," he said.

"What time does the Anne Frank House close?" she asked. "Maybe we could go there now."

"Not sure. Let's see."

But it turned out that the Anne Frank House sold tickets only online—it said so on the doors around the side—and when Jack checked on his phone he discovered it was booked up for two weeks. "Dammit. But it says they release some tickets every day. We'll try tomorrow. I guess we should have done some research."

"Never," she said, because they never did, not ahead of time. Never consulted a guidebook, combed through a website (except for accommodation). They were exactly the same in this respect, one of the pleasures of their life together, their love of happenstance. How, when traveling, they congratulated themselves on their luck!

They got a free tourist map from a nearby souvenir shop and examined the spiderweb of Central Amsterdam.

"We avoid *this*," said Jack, pointing to the center.

"But what if we want to go to a sex show?" she said.

"Ha ha."

But what if? she thought.

Sadie had somehow not bothered to imagine Amsterdam at all, beyond bicycles and picturesque houses, though she had an image in her head of the red-light district left over from high school: a friend had gone to Amsterdam and said she'd passed the prostitutes in their windows, which Sadie had imagined as ordinary residential windows, with sashes; she could see women in their lingerie leaning, resting their breasts on the sills.

They walked along the canal, past little design stores and souvenir shops and bars. The sunset was peachy, blue, a parfait, perfect. Every bar was their ideal bar. They passed a lit-up grocery store and went in to get supplies and walked out, swinging the white plastic bags on their wrists. They crossed again in front of the Anne Frank House.

"We'll crack you!" said Jack, and then, "Jesus, listen to the man." He stopped. "Do you feel different?"

"Different how?"

"Different married."

"Oh, that. No," she said.

"I do."

"That's because your parents are alive."

He didn't say anything to that.

"Poor Thomas," said Sadie suddenly. "Poor Robin." Robin was Thomas's twin brother.

"Poor all of us," said Jack.

There was a liquor store around the corner, selling mulled wine dispensed from the sort of stainless-steel suburban samovar that Sadie remembered from elementary school functions. "This is very good," the liquor-store proprietor promised them, working the spigot. He was in his forties, with a saddlebag goatee, wider at the bottom. "This will make you love each other truly."

"What if we already love each other truly?" asked Jack.

"Why, I don't know," said the shopkeeper. "You'd be the first instance in my shop."

The walls were lined with bottles. Jack pulled a Dutch liqueur from a shelf. "My father would appreciate this place," he said, and just then an American man walked in, looked around, and said, "Do you sell bread?"

"Do I sell bread?" the shopkeeper said. "Do I sell *bread*? Look around you, man! What sort of place do you believe you have found yourself in? No, no, don't go away, you're in luck. We have here on exhibition a mythical creature: the man and wife in truly love with each other. Look!" said the shopkeeper. "Marvel!"

"I love my wife," said the bread-seeking American.

"No," said the liquor-store owner, "you don't."

In the middle of the night Sadie jolted awake. It took a moment to realize that the dark, dazzled field she was looking at was the surface of the canal. Nobody was on the street in front of the Anne Frank House. Wait. Here came a man and woman, walking along, no idea that Sadie was watching. She felt like a character in a European movie: perhaps the couple would dance. Perhaps one would murder the other, then toss the body into the canal. They kept on without talking. She looked at the water. A glittering something floated winkingly along the surface, sparkling, Tinker Bell gone for a dip—no, a slowly turning plastic bottle.

She'd lied: she did feel different married, in an entirely practical way. For all the years of their life together, they'd never fully merged their finances—she'd arrived with debts, student and credit card, of which she'd felt ashamed, and burdened by—and she'd had a series of jobs, never particularly lucrative: working at oddball magazine after oddball magazine, writing for an alternative alternative newspaper— the actual alternative newspaper, the good one, had folded years ago—and lately she was teaching editing at Bunker Hill Community College. Jack had tenure at BU, and was kindly, and paid for most things. She hated the kindliness. Perhaps they would apply for joint everything, but no matter: now, if they divorced, she could get some of his money. She had no plans to, but she wondered at the thought of it. They were family now. She could demand things of him, because they were also hers.

"Goddammit," said Jack in the morning, sitting on a white chair in the white kitchen, peering at his phone.

"What's the matter?"

"Fucking Anne Frank," he said to be funny, then thought better of it, *"House.* I'm about the thousandth in line to buy tickets for today." He showed her the screen. It had a little animation of a stick figure walking.

"That doesn't sound promising."

"It doesn't. I already bought tickets for the Van Gogh

Museum for later today. Everything's timed. Shall I make you a coffee, darling?"

"Yes please." She picked up her book and read it while Jack stared at his phone and made a coffee in the little humming coffee maker. The book had been recommended by a friend, and Sadie found it simultaneously fascinating and boring, a near and mere transcript of life. She wasn't sure she hated the book, but she hated books like it, though she'd never read any of them—they were international, these books, Norwegian and English and Irish and Canadian, novels in which people bought coffee and had long conversations and felt sorry for themselves and reached no conclusions. How we live now, if by *we* you meant white people without much in the way of money problems. She, Sadie, was one of those. Perhaps if she had read it at home, she would have been riveted. Or perhaps she *was* riveted: she kept picking it up to read it, to see if anything had happened while she'd been away, she missed it in a way she didn't miss other books.

"You want milk in this?" Jack asked.

"I got cream," she said.

"I am sorry to report," said Jack, "that you got buttermilk."

"Oh. I should have known. Milk's great, thank you."

"God*dam*mit," said Jack, looking at his phone.

In the Van Gogh Museum, Sadie leaned on the wall and declared, "This whole city is pitching." It was a new shining building, crammed with people, near the Rijksmuseum. The boat *did* move, it turned out, a gentle rocking from side to side, barely noticeable on board, which got into your own personal canals and knocked you off balance later.

"I think we were lucky to get tickets," said Jack.

"I might have to sit down. You don't feel it?"

He tilted his head, to think, to recalibrate his inner ear. "No."

They hadn't realized that the paintings in the Van Gogh Museum were displayed in chronological order, and they accidentally started at the top, at the very end, not at Van Gogh's death but at his brother Theo's, who'd died months after Vincent's suicide, in an asylum.

"I hadn't known that," said Sadie. "I thought he was the steady one."

"Me too," said Jack. He thought of Thomas—it seemed foolish to have come here, all things considered—and also of Thomas's twin, Robin, who'd come to their wedding but had left before the meal. A nice man, Robin: ordinary, as Thomas had never been.

Everyone had been so devastated by Thomas's death, Jack felt he should lock up his own sorrow. There was something in him that always deferred to other people in this way, he measured his own grief and found it smaller, something that could be attended to later: he had a cactus soul, he sometimes thought—it needed water, too, but it could wait. When Sadie's mother died of course he deferred to Sadie; when Fiona died, to his parents, and to Piet; when Thomas died to everyone in the family but then, too, to Sadie. His own grief was larded with helplessness, with the certainty that he was wrong to live so far from his family, that he had abdicated his position accidentally. The wedding had helped with that, but that was past, and he felt now with the force of a premonition worry over Robin, Robin the ordinary, Robin the sturdy. Robin worked for an estate agent in the Cotswolds, and Jack wanted to pull up his Facebook page to make sure he was okay. He got his phone out.

"Not here," said Sadie. "Let's just look at the art for now. Do you think we should start at the beginning?"

"No," said Jack. "Let's fight the current."

Stick to your mistake. They rewound Van Gogh's life. The colors got more ordinary. A certain uninteresting prettiness asserted itself. A child was born, and then another.

There was nothing alarming on Robin's Facebook page, once Jack checked, but also nothing recent. He tried the Anne Frank House again. He was 276 in line, better, even hopeful, though soon enough he got the same message, that tickets were sold out and he should try again later. He waited in line for the Anne Frank House at the Monday market; at the Café de Prins, where they drank beer and ate bitterballen. He waited when they accidentally walked into the edge of the red-light district, and he didn't even notice: they were going to see the Oude Kerk and passed by a bunch of women in their windows, a whole row curving around the back of the church. Not the ordinary second-story windows that Sadie had imagined, leaning as though in kissing booths, but plate-glass windows at ground level, so you could see all of them in their platonically ideal lingerie, bustiers, stockings,

garters—human women, just like her. Once she had seen a
pigeon at a zoo, looking at an emu. Jack was poking at his
phone. He waited online at dinner at a café devoted to the
memory of a 1930s singer who had clearly been very famous
in the Netherlands: every wall covered in pictures of him,
black-and-white, his mouth open, his eyes sorrowful at his
words but filled with pleasure at the sound of his own voice;
below on the checked tablecloth little wooden boats of may-
onnaise sailed to the edge of the map. He waited online at
breakfast, at the Rembrandt House—where you could just
walk in, and which, like all of dry land, heaved around Sadie. She wanted to go back to the boat, to read, to drink wine,
to peer out at Amsterdam.

The way Jack looked at his phone reminded her of the
bad few years, a decade before, when he'd suddenly become
obsessed with scratch tickets, a dedicated niche problematic
gambler. What he liked was to hold the scratch ticket in one
hand, a quarter in the other, and concentrate. Suspense, but
not too much. Occasional reward, enough to keep you going, to reinvest. He spent thousands of dollars two bucks
at a time. His money, his money entirely, she couldn't say
anything, but she did. "You have to stop!" "I know." "This
isn't like you." He might remember to throw away the spent
tickets (though he had to check them again to make sure he
really had, he *had* lost), but the material he scratched off—
what was it called? what was it made of? was it safe to in-
hale? on the tickets it looked silver but rubbed off it was
gray—it was everywhere, excretory, *snotty*.

Now he looked at his phone with the same arrogant hope,

the same handsome panic, as though whatever happened would prove his worth, at least for the next twenty-four hours.

So many shop windows in Amsterdam were pleasing at a distance but dizzying close-up, whole windows of Delft: tiles, mugs, clogs, towering tulip vases, figurines. There was no better blue, but even it couldn't make everything classy.

"I like the rabbit," said Jack.

"Who, Miffy?"

"The rabbit."

"The rabbit with the *X*ed-out mouth," she said.

"Those're whiskers, surely."

"Miffy," she said. "The bunny rabbit's name."

"You don't like it."

"It's twee," she said.

"It's not!"

"Bit twee."

"You're an American. You don't even know what twee is."

"*You're* an American," she said. Then, "Okay, what does it mean?"

"It's—it's like wet," he said. "To describe somebody who's dim. Americans don't know what wet means because you're *all* wet."

"*You're* all wet," she said. "You're all *twee*. Prezzies," she said. "Sammies. Mozzies. The English are twee," she said suddenly and with passion. She had never believed in anything so deeply. She had hated tweeness her entire life, the cutesy, the sweet, the things that could not wound you. She'd rather be an idiot than twee. "You have to be from a small country to be twee. I'm from a large one. You like *puppets*," she said accusingly.

"All right," he said. "Okay. It's all right." He put his arm around her, and they started walking. "I don't want to go back to America."

"Me neither. I have to work Monday."

"God," said Jack, whose semester did not start for weeks. "I wish I knew what to do. Where to live."

"Live where you live," she said. "With your wife."

"Yes with you," he said. He got his phone out again. He thought about calling his sister Katie, the twins' mother, but he couldn't figure out what to say: she did not need his premonitions. He pulled up the Anne Frank House website— they were passing in front of it, and maybe there would be a last-minute, end-of-the-day ticket.

"Can we sit a minute?" he said.

"It might not happen," said Sadie.

"You have to believe it'll happen."

"It's okay if it doesn't."

"It's not!" he said. He looked at the grand modern entrance they'd built onto the nineteenth-century Dutch one. A glass front with heavy doors, the new and pristine lobby visible. Anything Anne Frank had touched was hidden.

There was nobody waiting in line to get in with their timed tickets, just a young bespectacled guard with a walkie-talkie strapped to her shoulder. A father approached with his daughter. The daughter was ten, perhaps, or eleven, and seemed to have dressed herself in a way that in a few years would seem louche on her but now looked like a costume: mismatched socks, Mary Janes, black pants, a piebald cardigan falling off one shoulder, a beret. She looked bookish and doomed; she was just coming into glamour. The guard shrugged and smiled.

The father was speaking English. Jack could just hear him, gesturing to his daughter—*little girl, end of day, any chance?* The guard hesitated, then held up a single finger and began to confer with the walkie-talkie on her shoulder. You could see the man and child take each other's hands to silently tell each other, *Hold still. It might happen. It could happen. We only had to ask.*

No.

Jack said it aloud—"No"—and then he stood. If it were possible, if exceptions were to be made—

The guard glanced up and saw Jack and turned to the father. With great regret, she shook her head.

"I'm sorry." She gestured at the encroaching Jack. "You understand."

"Oh no!" said the little girl. Already she was assembling a stoic expression, the sort that takes muscle, to hold back her tears. She was a well-brought-up child. She straightened her crooked cardigan, took off her hat, and examined the inside. For God's sake, she even had a notebook under her arm.

"Thanks for ruining it," the father said to Jack.

"I didn't ruin it!" said Jack.

"You ruined it," the man said darkly. "You did. You ruined it."

Sadie and Jack crossed the garbage bridge in silence. He fidgeted with the key on its wooden block. "You *did* ruin it," said Sadie quietly.

The liquor store was shut up. The Cheese Museum was in full swing.

"Let's go out to dinner," said Jack.

"I want to read my book."

"You hate that book."

"That's right, I do."

"We can try again tomorrow. You have to see it."

"I *don't*."

"You do."

"Hand to God, the way you want me to see the Anne Frank House is starting to feel anti-Semitic." She regretted saying it instantly, which was how she knew it was true. Not his feeling, but hers.

"That's not funny," he said.

"I know," she said, with a dreadful smile on her face.

"Sadie," said Jack, "I want to have a child."

At first she thought he meant, *I am leaving you.* But it was more preposterous and heartbreaking than that. He'd always been more bourgeois than she was.

"Let's do it," he said. "Let's just—let's get carried away on our honeymoon."

"It doesn't work that way."

"Why *not*?"

"Human biology doesn't work that way. It's not—I'm about to get my period."

"So let's stop it," he said.

"Do you know anything about women's bodies?"

"You're mean," he said. "It's not too late. For a child. We are at a fork in the road."

They began to walk toward their boat. They were holding hands. She felt, with great certainty, that the road had already forked. She could not back up. Two roads diverged in a wood, and she had missed the divergence, gone bumbling on, and that was fine.

"You don't want a baby," she said. "Your *parents* want a baby. You're too old to care so much about what they want."

He dropped her hand and strode ahead to the boat. All week he'd slowed his pace to hers, she realized now. When she caught up, he was unlocking the hatch, but furiously—she worried he'd drop the key in the canal. "That is not fair," he said, "that's not fair, that's not fair." There had to be a better phrase. "That is *so* not fair." He pulled the hatch up. "Go ahead," he told her, and she went down the little ladder the forbidden way, facing forward, so that she didn't have to look up at him. She grabbed her book and took herself straight to the bedroom, slid herself onto the bed like a book herself, turned on the lamp with its elf-cap shade, and began to read in her usual state of irritation, my *God*, nothing would *ever* happen in this book, maybe she should chuck it into the canal, and she was at first only dimly aware of the sound of the hatch lowering, and the padlock clucking shut, but a different sound from usual, because it was clucking from the outside.

Jack had locked her in.

Well, he thought, once he'd closed the hasp and slid it home, that, maybe, maybe that is anti-Semitic. His phone rang. He assumed it was Sadie, realizing what he'd done: he'd locked his wife in a boat to punish her for being insufficiently interested in Anne Frank. For being insufficiently interested in his feelings. It was a malady of marriage. His malady, he understood. Maybe he could give the boat a kick and send it down the canal, off to the low countries, whatever those were. The phone was ringing. He answered it.

"It's Katie," said his youngest older sister. She was crying. He hoped it was one of his parents, knew it was not.

Inside the boat, Sadie thought, *I am not a vengeful person, but*. It was six o'clock the day before they were to fly home. How could they salvage this trip? This *honeymoon*? She could see people across the canal. Eventually—if he did not come back (he would come back)—she could open the window and call for help. The very thought of it made her feel shy, and the shyness turned to anger. *I am not a vengeful person*, she told herself, and she opened the window, the porthole. She decided to send a message. The first thing would be his underpants, she told herself, striped orange, knit, she was very fond of them, *pants*, Jack called them, there were certain things he could only call by their English names, things essential to childhood, pants and trousers and biscuits and pudding. Should she throw out his things piece by piece, or all at one time? *Do your best*, she told herself.

But then there was Jack at the foot of the bed, his cell phone in the flat of his hands. She could not interpret the look on his face. "You're kidding me," she said, because what else could the phone mean? But he shook his head. She let go of the underpants. She went to her husband.

———

She loved puppets, too, of course she did. Before, and during, and even after, she loved them, those dear beings—twee, of course they were, which was what made them dear—who died of abandonment over and over. And then were resurrected.

ACKNOWLEDGMENTS

I owe much gratitude to many people:

The title "Two Sad Clowns" is taken from an illustration by my great good friend Marguerite White, with whom I have been talking about art and other things for nearly forty years. I thank her for that and so much more.

Everyone at Ecco, especially Helen Atsma, Daniel Halpern, Miriam Parker, Sonya Cheuse, Allison Saltzman, and Sara Birmingham.

Everyone at Dunow, Carlson, and Lerner, especially Henry Dunow, who has been my agent and dear pal for thirty years.

Megan Lynch, for early faith in this book; my colleagues, particularly Lisa Olstein and Deb Olin Unferth; Catherine Nichols for last-minute name assistance; Lisa Sweasy of Venthaven, for an interview about the late Jimmy Nelson that inspired a story.

Jonathan Green and Elizabeth Gallant Green, for shelter in any number of storms.

Arno, Claudia, and Callum Nauwels provided some notable architecture, Irish and Dutch.

Søren Lind and the Brecht Hus, for inspiration and lodging in Denmark.

Yiyun Li, with much love and gratitude for ineffable things, amid all the words.

Paul Lisicky and Ann Patchett, as usual, read this manuscript and were enormously helpful, kind, and generous. Scott Heim read these stories and gave me irreplaceable help, from sentence to paragraph to story.

Thanks to my family—including my brother, Harry, and his wife, Marie Domingo. My lovely in-laws—Mary Harvey and the late Simon Harvey; the late James Harvey; Simon, Catherine, Charlie, and Henrietta Burchell; Nicholas, Marie-Ange, Elfreda, and Oscar Harvey—resemble no fictional in-laws contained in this book.

Gus and Matilda Harvey are the children I would have invented for myself if my imagination were good enough.

To Edward Carey I owe debts, both literary and otherwise, that I have never successfully put into words.

"Proof," "Mistress Mickle All at Sea," "A Walk-Through Human Heart," "Birdsong from the Radio," and "It's Not You" were originally published in *Zoetrope All-Story* (with many thanks, as always, to Michael Ray). "Mistress Mickle All at Sea" and "It's Not You" were published in *The Pushcart Prize: Best of the Small Presses*, edited by Bill Henderson. "It's Not You" was published in *Best American Short Stories 2020* (with thanks to Curtis Sittenfeld and Heidi Pitlor). "Birdsong from the Radio" was written for the anthology *xo*

Orpheus: Fifty New Myths, edited by Kate Bernheimer; it was reprinted in *The O. Henry Prize Stories 2015*, with thanks to Marissa Colón Margolies, Taylor Flory Ogletree, and Laura Furman. "Robinson Crusoe at the Waterpark" was originally published in *Reader, I Married Him: Stories Inspired by Jane Eyre*, edited by Tracy Chevalier.